Praise for
Feather and Bone
by Lazlo Strangolov

"Transylvania's melange of sights, sounds and (especially) smells is conveyed with a humour which is unfadingly black and in a tone where tongue is permanently in cheek. Hilarious."
Books for Keeps

"Exciting, gruesome and genuinely scary. In the hands of Strangolov, the question of 'what's lurking in the dark wood' is no longer a cliché."
Norwich Evening News

"What he has written is extraordinary [...] Strangolov creates a sense of menace and unease."
Literary Review

"The humour throughout is darkest black, the style totally tongue-in-cheek and the whole concept hilarious: all very clever – but not for the squeamish or for anyone with an allergy to poultry or associated odours."
Robert Dunbar, *The Irish Times*

"Here's a book with a difference... Wow! What a story! And such powerful illustrations. Lazlo's random pencil doodles are scribbled over the text – an inspired touch. It's absolutely wonderful."

Reviewer's Choice, *Your Bookshelf*

"This is a really unusual story, it is a page-turner with darkly comic events that will have you amazed at the way the story unfolds. You won't be disappointed by this book, just take my word for it."

Reader review, *First News*

"Exploding rabbits, spooked chickens and things that go chop in the night... [A] gloriously scary children's book."

Glasgow Evening Times

"A modern fable very much styled on the Mid-European folk tales made popular by the Brothers Grimm and Hans Christian Andersen."

First News

"A book written for the boys, and I'm sure that they will love the final outcome to the mystery!"

Write Away

Lazlo Strangolov's Tooth and Claw

ghost writing from the underground

WATERFORD CITY AND COUNTY LIBRARIES WITHDRAWN

WALKER BOOKS

WATERFORD CITY AND
WITHDRAWN
LIBRARIES
Leabharlann Chonndae
Phortláirge

This book is dedicated
to the dogs

budgie?
baboon?
beaver?
→ BEAGLE! ←

A FOREWORD OF WARNING
BY THE AUTHOR

In a spa town close to me, but a world away from you, there lives a very sad girl indeed. Usually so cheery by nature, Lumina Lupesco's heart has just been broken. A most tragic event is responsible. One that every pet owner dreads.

Spiral down with me now through the twilight mist to a plot of land behind that cottage near the square. There, we find her before an open grave. Little Lumin's father stands across from her. He holds a spade with both hands. Grim-faced, Mister Lupesco awaits her nod before beginning the task of laying the family dog to rest.

"I'll miss you, Scud," she says, her voice weak

with grief and tears. "I'll miss you more than you can imagine."

Without a word, her father drops the first load of soil into the hole. The dog's wrecked and mangled body is wrapped in a cotton sheet. The soil makes contact with a dull thud. Several hours earlier, Lumin and her father had heard a similar sound from the lane. That time, it had been preceded by a horn and an urgent squeal of brakes.

"I feel responsible," says Mister Lupesco. "I should've fixed the gate weeks ago."

"It's nobody's fault," the girl insists. "Not even the driver of the truck. Scud never did have much road sense. As a beagle, he loved the thrill of a good chase."

Her father smiles, reflecting on the dog's habit of haring blindly after squirrels and wild rabbits. "Scud was one of a kind," he says, and continues his sorry task. "Nothing can replace him."

Come bedtime, all that Lumina can think about is her loss. Memories of her years with Scud continue to float in and out of her mind. Her pillow is wet with tears. Underneath it, she has stowed a photograph of her beloved dog. The image has faded over time. Her father had taken it on the day Scud first toddled into her life. He sported stumpy legs, large, pleading eyes and floppy ears that could've been cut

Poor Lumina

from felt. Little Lumin had fallen in love with him immediately. From that moment on, the pair had become inseparable.

Unable to sleep, she rises to peek through the curtains and look out upon the grave. There it is under moonlight, marked by a wooden cross. Her father hammered it together in the outbuilding among the lava rock at the rear of the plot. After dark, in this space that doubles as a library and workshop, he would often retire to reflect on life, make repairs or research his interests in anatomy and alchemy. Despite the late hour, a candle lamp is glowing inside the outbuilding's single window. Little Lumin does not notice him at his workbench, such is the focus of her thoughts. Mister Lupesco sees her up there, however. Her presence draws him from the idle calculations he's been making in his notebook, and it weighs heavily on his conscience. Scud had transformed his daughter's life. Ever since he had presented her with the puppy, soon after her mother faded away, she had gone from being quiet and introverted to the blooming flower adored by everyone.

"I can't afford to lose you too," he says to himself, and sets down his pen. "Scud was your heart and soul."

Loosening his spotted neckerchief, Mister Lupesco contemplates the grave. Where the earth has settled, he notices that the cross is sunken to one side. It's as if the spirit of the poor dog six feet under had made an attempt to burrow his way out. Aware that his daughter has returned to her bed, he steps out under the stars to straighten the cross. As he does so, a notion enters his mind. It is both unthinkable and bewitching, and causes him to freeze.

A moment later, having rolled up his sleeves for the second time that day, he returns to the workshop to collect his spade.

Friends, we find this desperate tale unfolding amid foothills that are highly regarded in my country. It is some distance from the capital, in a spa town celebrated for her hot springs. Here, the groundwater that bubbles up through fissures in the rock has been *super*heated. Geologically-speaking, the place is closer than most to the molten magma layers that flow beneath the earth's surface. Some say the locals might as well be living on a hob plate, but for them it is home. Where you might expect to find a fountain at the centre of the town's square, there is instead a puddle that appears to be coming to the boil. You would be wise to stand well back, however, for every twenty minutes and twelve seconds precisely this celebrated geyser throws a magnificent head of steam high into the air.

It is not the only landmark, of course. Beyond the rooftops, among the forested slopes overlooking the town, stands the geothermal power station. It is a brooding, windowless hulk of a building, clad in pipes and shrouded in steam. You may agree it is not pretty. Then again, it is the source of the spa town's hot water and electricity. Nothing goes to waste in the process. The naturally heated water drawn from deep below must be stripped of silt and minerals before it can feed the supply. Once extracted, this sulphurous sludge might stink of rotten eggs and yet it is said to possess miraculous restorative properties. For this reason, it is piped out of the power station and dumped into what is the region's greatest attraction: an artificial lagoon.

This kidney-shaped pool is the centrepiece of a health clinic that stands within the shadow of the great power station. Should you suffer any skin condition, from sores and scales to boils and blackheads, or simply feel tired and run down, a wallow in her warm, pungent but milky-blue waters is the surest way to leave you feeling ten years younger. The sludge isn't only pumped into the lagoon, of course. All manner of beauty products, remedies and therapies are cooked up by the scientists in the clinic's laboratory, which is where Lumina's father prepares to head for work the next morning.

"The worst is over," he assures his daughter at their cottage door. "Things can only get better from here. Just think! This is your last day of term. You have the holidays ahead of you. Plenty of time to … to…" And there his reasoning fades away.

Lumina is a pretty child. With her heart-shaped face and freckled cheeks, she brings sunshine to her father's life throughout the darkest months. Just seeing her so down leaves him feeling helpless and adrift.

"Things will never be the same again," Lumina replies glumly, and hands him the sandwiches she always makes for his lunch. "But even without Scud, life must go on."

Throughout his working day at the laboratory, Mister Lupesco has only to remind himself how resigned his daughter seemed. It's enough to convince him that he is doing the right thing. It might involve borrowing several test tubes of mineral extract in its purest, most restricted form, but the modification he has in mind is his only chance to restore little Lumin's happiness.

That night, on peeping through her bedroom curtains, Lumin notes that the cross marking Scud's grave is standing upright once again. Dark and clotted clouds are massing overhead. On occasion, they flash and flicker faintly from within. Despite the absence of any moonshine, the lamp burning brightly inside her father's workshop casts a clear light across her beagle's resting place. Seeing this, Lumin takes heart in the fact that Scud is there to watch over him in spirit. It's a thought she carries to bed with her. There, wrung out by this tragic turn of events, she finds the sleep she so desperately needs.

Such is her exhaustion that she does not stir when the storm breaks in the early hours. As the rain begins to lash the earth, not even the sound of sawing and then hammering is enough to raise her. Had she awoken, thrown a coat over her head and crept out to investigate, she might've been drawn to the window of her father's workshop. Despite the fug on the inside of the glass, obscuring her view of his worktop, perhaps she would have noted the concentration in his eyes. This would have surely intensified as he finished his needlework and drew a very special mixture into a stainless-steel syringe. Even if she had witnessed all this, no doubt Lumin would've shrunk away when he raised the needle high and prepared to plunge it deep into the heart of whatever was laid out before him.

Had she dared to look back, starting at a nearby lightning strike, she would most certainly have seen the expression on his face switch from concern to surprise and then outright elation.

"Life goes on … life goes on!"

But all this is a fancy, of course, for Mister Lupesco's little girl sleeps through until dawn. With the storm long gone, only the sound of birdsong can be heard outside. Having dreamed about poor Scud throughout the night, it is easy for her to recall how the beagle would always bound in at first thing and eagerly paint her face with slobber. With her eyes still shut, dozing still, she can almost feel his paws pinning her shoulders as his tongue slaps her neck and cheek. Then she hears the trace sound of a playful whine, so close to her ear that it cannot be in her mind. Above all, it is the mouldering, eggy smell that persuades her to lift one eyelid, and then snap bolt upright with a gasp.

From the doorway, an exhausted Mister Lupesco looks on with a smile. The moment is both miraculous and touching. It also completes the foundation for a tale best continued by the girl reunited with a dog back from the dead.

Layla Strangelov

The Bunker
Romania
(exact location undisclosed)

1

Today, as the holidays stretch out before me, I feel as if I have been reborn. Every time I think about what my father has achieved, I look at dear Scud to be sure I am not mistaken.

"How did you do it?" I ask, but he will say only that he had struck lucky.

"The fact is, your dog is at your side once more," he adds. "Even so, we should not celebrate too soon. Like any pet that has travelled from distant shores, we really must keep him here in quarantine. Just until we are sure he has not brought back anything unpleasant."

3

♥   ♥   ♥

Although dear Scud appears a little different, it is most certainly him. I can see it in his one remaining eye: a gleam he possessed as a puppy, which I feared had gone for ever when we found him sprawled across the skid trail left by the truck. It may glow red like an ember now, but I can still see his soul in there.

My father has battled hard to patch him up. The stitching across his lost eye is neat and tidy, as is the bandaging around his rear quarters. One hind-leg may be twisted around the wrong way, but he is able to hobble, trot and turn in circles of excitement around me. That the gristly tip of his tail is exposed doesn't seem to bother my beagle one bit. He can still wag it madly whenever I pay him attention. I don't mind that Scud's bones click when he moves. I also understand why he's somewhat spongy in the flesh. Even though he was only buried for a short time, the heightened temperature undoubtedly accelerated the decomposition process. I am thankful to my father for bringing him back before things went too far. My dog may be somewhat squishy now; I just tell myself it makes for a more rewarding cuddle.

What I need to get used to is the trace of sulphur I can smell in Scud's fur. It's like he's endlessly breaking wind through his skin pores. I washed him down straight away, with a bucket of hot water and tar soap, but it didn't shift the niff at all. As for his bark,

4

I'm hoping that will come back in time. Earlier, when the post flopped through the letterbox, Scud rushed towards it sounding more like a rattlesnake than a dog. It's a most unsettling wheeze, backed up by the sound of snapping jaws, but for now that is enough. My fine boy is back with me, and I cannot stop smiling.

"Yesterday, at school," I admit to my father, "I couldn't bring myself to tell anyone what had happened. Maybe deep down I just did not believe that he was dead."

"Your silence might be a blessing," he says. "How else are we going to explain his continued existence?"

"It's certainly a miracle."

I rock up onto my tiptoes, kiss my father on the cheek, and thank him for what he has done. My father merely flattens his lips and nods. Next, he glances at the dog, before leaving me to collect something from the larder. Scud knows that he has a treat in store, for his tail begins to switch back and forth.

I try to ignore the sound that accompanies this motion – like someone repeatedly cracking the knuckles in their fingers.

"This should keep him busy," my father says, emerging now with a shinbone from the mutton we had stewed the week before. "Here you go, boy."

Crouching down before Scud, he places the offering at his paws. Normally, my dog would take it to his corner and gnaw it for hours on end. This time, he creeps forward to sniff it before collecting it between his jaws and heading between us for the back door.

"What's he up to?" I wonder out loud.

Scud scratches at the door, whining in a whisper. I let him out and watch from the threshold with my father as he struggles across the grass.

"I think I know," my father says next and chuckles to himself. "He's just being a dog. A regular dog like any other."

With the bone between his teeth, Scud approaches his own grave. I know now it is unoccupied, which makes me feel a little easier when my dog drops his prize and begins to burrow into the earth. As the loose soil sprays across the grass, I turn to my father and beam at him.

"At least he'll remember where it's buried," I say. "Though I don't suppose that either of us will forget this moment."

"Promise me you will not breathe a word," he replies. "Bringing back the dead is a feat I never wish to repeat. It goes against the way of things, Lumin, but then you are my daughter and your happiness is all that matters to me. Once Scud is fit to leave the cottage, we should pretend the accident never happened. Is that understood?"

I look back at my dog. He has dug so deep that only his tail is visible.

"But he only has one eye now," I point out. "And he smells strange."

"All dogs pong," my father replies. "And plenty get into nasty scrapes. He stops there, smiles to himself and winks at me. "Scud might be scarred but life goes on, eh? As it does for us all. That's why the clinic must never know. If word got out that I had taken restricted samples from the lab, my job would be for the chop."

In all the excitement following

Scud's resurrection, I realize I have forgotten to prepare my father his sandwiches. I make them every day, even during the holidays, and take pride in the fact that he has never gone hungry at work. With this in mind, I butter some bread, slice a cold sausage and lay it out with beetroot and watercress. Having wrapped it up in greaseproof paper, I grab an apple from the bowl to go with it and set off for the clinic.

Shortly after leaving our cottage, I find a crack has opened up across the lane. It would be too small to notice, but for the escaping steam. This is not an unusual sight around here. Everyone knows about the activity deep beneath our feet. All that heat has to escape somewhere. If it isn't drawn up by the power station, it rises to the surface through fissures in the ground rock. Sometimes it causes problems, but that is a hazard of living in this spa town. A little further down the lane, I pass two cottages with a plot between them which is basically a steaming hole full of rubble. Some time ago, another cottage used to be squashed in here. It belonged to Gertruda Gašper, the clinic's head masseuse. The chickens she kept in a coop out the back displayed the first sign that something wasn't right. Over the course of a fortnight, every egg she collected from their nest turned out to be hard boiled inside the shell.

Then the steam began to creep up through a gap between the floorboards.

At first it only affected her kitchen. It meant the windows were permanently fogged up on the inside. Things became more serious when a crack crept out across the wall in her hallway. Within a day, it spread from one side of the ceiling to the other. Over the next few nights, poor Gertruda would wake up in a sweat and find herself adrift in a sea of fog. When it became too hot to pad around the ground floor in bare feet, she finally sought advice. Following an inspection by several local builders, the masseuse begrudgingly but hurriedly packed her bags and took

10

up residence in one of the clinic's guest-rooms.

Six days later, on the cusp of daybreak, the neighbours awoke to the creak and crash of Gertruda Gašper's cottage collapsing. The foundations had quite literally boiled away. By rights, such a catastrophe should have turned this place into a ghost town. Why would anyone in their right mind want to live one degree away from disaster? Well, like those residents of hamlets perched on crumbling cliffs, this is the place we have always called home. Speaking for myself, I have no doubt that Scud will forewarn me in good time, should a bad thing look set to happen.

Dogs have a fine sixth sense, and I am sure that a spell in the grave has not put paid to that.

"Hey, Lumin! Poor you." The voice of sympathy comes from the other side of the lane. I look around to see a lady who would intimidate me greatly if I did not know her as a family friend. "I heard about your sad news. The driver of the truck told me everything."

"He did?" I say with some alarm. "Oh."

Petra Appollonio is tall as a willow and ever so elegant. The most striking thing about her, however, is something we all try not to notice. Petra once trod the catwalks in the fashion houses of the capital. Today, on account of a catastrophic chemical skin-peeling treatment by a rogue cosmetic surgeon, she

11

lives with a livid burn on one side of her face. I am used to it now. I know that Petra is no different on the inside. Still, should she stand before you in a manner that hides her disfigurement and then turn the other way, it can look like two different women have been stitched together. Right now, she's facing me directly with an expression hovering between sadness and pity.

"Shortly after the accident," she tells me, "I found the poor man pulled up in tears outside my cottage.

PETRA APPOLONIC

Naturally, I took him inside for a cup of sweet tea. It sounds like an awful business."

With her are half a dozen beagles. These are her "angels", as she calls them collectively. All of them are rescue dogs from the shelter she set up with her compensation money. None strain to move on. The pack simply sits there patiently. They are so grateful to Petra for giving them a chance in life that she is able to hold their leads between her thumb and forefinger. She does so with her arm tipped up at the elbow and her wrist on full display. It is an elegant pose that comes naturally to her.

I clear my throat, struggling to hold her gaze. "My dog is at peace," I say, which is not entirely a lie, for I'd left Scud out cold upon his bed in the kitchen corner.

Petra Appollonio regards me for a moment in such a way that I think I might even tell her the truth. I want to admit that my father dug up my dog, slow-cooking in his grave, and breathed fresh life into him. I am desperate to share the news that he had done so by concocting a potion capable of kick-starting a cold heart. I feel *sure* that I can tell her, in fact. Then I remind myself of the consequences should word spread, and reach out to pet her dogs.

"If there is anything my angels and I can do for you," says Petra after a moment, "all you have to do is let me know."

"You are very kind," I tell her, standing tall again. Petra continues to regard me as if searching for something behind my eyes. I begin to back away. "If you'll excuse me," I say, "I must deliver lunch to my father."

"Just be sure to give yourself some time to grieve," she replies, but I turn and keep on going. "I am watching you, Lumin. We all are."

It is the first day of our spring break. Snow remains on the uppermost reaches of the mountains, but nothing ever settles here in the foothills. Even when a blizzard sweeps across town, the heat beneath our feet quickly turns it to water.

Whenever the weather is bleak, there is only one place to be, and that is the lagoon. Even on this bright and clear day, as I approach the gates to the clinic that fronts it, the steam billowing up behind the roof reminds me how warm and comforting the water can be. It is hotter than a bath, but not enough to scald, while the mineral salts help the most bloated bodies stay buoyant. It means you can float on your back and close your eyes, even when the temperature has dropped below zero and the sleet is horizontal. The sense of peace is absolute, but for the constant hum from the power station. Sometimes it can feel like a living, breathing beast, especially when you know there's nobody inside. The operation is monitored remotely by the authorities, which adds to the sense of solitude. I love it here, as does everyone in this town. I try to come for a soak at least twice a week and consider myself to be a familiar face.

Which is why it comes as some surprise to be stopped as soon as I walk in. "May I see your membership card, Lumina? You know the rules."

This is Gertruda Gašper. The masseuse herself. I find her with the receptionist at the main desk. She's leafing through her reservations folder for the day. Gertruda is a stocky, formidable woman who always looks like she might overwhelm the white cotton tunic and trousers that all the staff must wear. Sometimes, when she wears her hair pulled tight in a bun, I can't help thinking she looks more like a sumo wrestler. When I produce my card, she peers at it over the half-moon spectacles she wears on a chain around her neck. Next she takes it from me for closer inspection. My heart begins to sink.

"I should like to see my father," I say and show her the sandwiches. "May I go through to the lab?"

Gertruda shakes her head, which is no surprise. I

GERTRUDA GAŠPER

look to the receptionist, who shrugs as if to say she doesn't have the authority to override the masseuse.

"This is the senior hour, as you well know. Unless you're over sixty, you can't come in."

"But I don't wish to use the facilities," I say pleadingly. "If my father doesn't get his sandwiches then he'll go hungry."

The receptionist looks at me with some pity, before returning to her paperwork. Gertruda hands me back my card. When I try to take it, she holds on to the corner long enough for me to meet her gaze.

"I dare say he'll survive," she says.

I glance at the receptionist. "May I leave them with you?"

The receptionist smiles and extends her hand, only for Gertruda to swat it away. "Leaving food-stuffs in the reception area goes against regulations," she declares, and promptly seizes the sandwiches for herself.

The moment the masseuse had sprung up from behind the desk, I knew that she would challenge me. Ever since her cottage had boiled away, throwing her life into chaos, Gertruda Gašper had earned a reputation as being a formidable enforcer of rules. Now that she had taken up residence in the spa itself, Gertruda had thrown herself into making sure that everything ran just as it should. Through her eyes, the slightest breach was unthinkable. It was as if she feared that it would cause the structure of her world to take another tumble. Even so, I can't help but appeal to her one more time.

"I made them myself," I say, and feel very uncomfortable when she begins to open up the package. "I guarantee they're no health hazard."

"Out of the question," she says. Before I can stop her, Gertruda peels away the top layer of bread and sniffs at the meat inside. Then she takes a slice of beetroot and pops it into her mouth. "What would Doctor Grubo say?"

The masseuse does not even glance at me as she

chews it between her back molars. It is only when her decision is questioned that she swallows hard and looks up with a start.

"Clearly you are unaware of Lumina's loss, Ms Gašper. I think it is only right that we make an exception here."

The man standing directly behind me is the clinic's founder and director, Doctor Grubo himself. I cannot be sure how long he has been there. All I know is that any mention of my dog at this time unsettles me.

"I don't mean to be a nuisance," I say, addressing everyone now. "I am simply here to bring my father his lunch."

Doctor Grubo is a picture of health. For a man approaching the autumn of his years, his tanning suggests many fine summers spent outdoors. Some say it's a result of numerous sessions on the spa's sunbed. One thing is for sure, however: the doctor is no slouch. Indeed, he still has elements of the physique that saw him win a national bodybuilding competition many years ago. I have heard dark mutterings that lately it isn't only the gym that maintains his impressive body but the use of highly illegal muscle-enhancing medication. Personally, I cannot believe a man of his standing would risk his reputation. Nor do I think he would gamble with the possibility of developing the moodswings and mania I am told

19

DR GRUB

can come from messing with such a shady science. Certainly he shows no sign of irritation at my presence. I just wish he would stop regarding me with such close attention.

"I was saddened to hear about your beagle," he says, fixing me with eyes as blue and vibrant as the lagoon itself. "As a boy I owned a pet python. Like Scud, it used to slip away frequently. One time it escaped and attempted to swallow a neighbour's rake." He pauses there, as if momentarily overwhelmed by the memory. "Needless to say, that didn't end well, but I can understand your pain, Lumina."

As he speaks, I stare at the floor. I do not dare lie to a man of such importance. "How did you know about Scud?" I ask in a voice so quiet I barely hear myself.

"The truck driver was on his way here when the collision occurred. We had a large order of spa products ready for collection." Doctor Grubo takes a moment to reply, clearly reflecting on the account the poor man must have given when he finally arrived. "I can only hope he made it back to the capital without further incident."

I feel my heart grow heavy. "If I may just visit my father," I say after a moment.

Doctor Grubo nods, ignoring the sharp intake of breath from behind the reception desk, and stands aside so I can pass. "Our thoughts are with you," he says.

I nod solemnly, feeling awful for keeping the truth to myself. As I leave the lobby, I catch Gertruda Gašper's eye. It is clear that she is simmering inwardly. Her lips have pursed as if pulled tight by invisible strings. On meeting my gaze, she nods to herself. Immediately I worry that the masseuse isn't only upset that I have bent the rules. The way

21

she is watching me, I fear she must know that Scud is still with us. With my head down now, I quicken my pace into the corridor.

Like the founder himself, the clinic is in impressive form for its age. The pine-clad walls are a little scuffed at the corners, but it's a bright, clean space that curves elegantly around one side of the lagoon. The overlooking gallery boasts windows that span from floor to ceiling. It affords a clear view of the lava rocks and the billowing steam. Every now and then, an aged body or a swim-capped head can be seen drifting blissfully in the healing waters. Visitors sometimes remark on how strange it is to be bathing in the shadow of such a monstrous-looking power station. As soon as they dip a toe into the water, however, they soon forget about it. I just wish that everyone would do the same about my dog.

"Lumina, what terrible news!"

"Poor child. Such a calamitous way to start the holidays."

Most of the staff know me by name. At this moment in time, I wish this was not the case. All I can do is hurry by the treatment rooms then clip down the spiral staircase that leads to the laboratory complex below. It is here that the clinic's many products are created. The range was once very popular throughout the country. Nowadays, the market is somewhat crowded. For this reason, the clinic strives to stay ahead of the game. The mineral extract may be unique to this region, but that is not always enough. Creating new products is key, even if it is a tweak to an existing formula. From facial scrubs with toadstool extract and tree bark shavings to eyelid serum containing no less than five per cent sparrow's egg yolk, everything is based on the minerals extracted from the cauldron beneath our feet, and then given a fresh spin. As a result of Doctor Grubo's tireless push for innovation, the clinic's range continues at least to be a popular draw in the capital's department stores. It is also the reason why my father and his colleagues are forced to work so hard.

"Aha, my sandwiches! Lumina, you are such a good girl."

24

I find my father at his bench. The rooms down here form a warren of sorts, with different areas for research, innovation, production, testing, packing and dispatch. I cannot begin to understand the nature of his work. The gas burners, beakers, bottles, crucibles, pipes, cylinders and containers tell me all I need to know.

"Everyone believes Scud is dead," I tell him urgently, keeping my voice down so as not to be overheard by any passing technician. "Word has spread around town and I don't know what to say!"

My father removes his safety goggles. "Say nothing," he advises me, having thought things through for a moment. "Once we're sure Scud has made a full recovery, we can simply make out that he's a new dog … which he is, in some ways," he adds.

I dwell on this for a moment. It isn't only his missing eye that I consider. "I suppose he looks a little different," I say finally.

"Exactly." My father ruffles my hair. "Cheer up, little Lumin! Your beloved Scud is back in the land of the living! You can leave the fretting to me."

I look up and try to read his face. "Is something troubling you?"

He draws breath to reply, only to hesitate for a moment. "Everything is fine," he says next. "And once we know that Scud is over the worst, everything will be even better."

I smile awkwardly, as does my father. I know he is just trying to stop me from worrying, but somehow his assurances have left me feeling even more uncomfortable.

"What is worse than dying?" I ask.

My father shrugs. This time, he offers no response.

On the way home, I am stopped by several school friends who offer me their condolences.

In response, I simply lower my eyes and press my lips together. I just cannot bring myself to pretend somehow that Scud has met his maker. My anxiety about the situation lasts all the way to our cottage. The last thing I want is for my father to get into trouble for what he has done. When I open the door, I realize what it is that will make me feel better. And that is a chance to wrap my arms around Scud.

"I still can't believe you're here!" I crinkle my nose as my dog licks my face. The sulphurous smell is really quite overpowering, as is the way the sinew and muscle beneath his heavily stitched skin still feels a bit squishy. I cannot help but squeeze him tight, and the sound of his organs rearranging themselves inside does not seem to bother Scud. When I gasp and let him go, he simply circles excitedly around me. "I suppose there's some way to go before you're fully healed," I decide. "Though I expect you're desperate to get out." At this, Scud stops before me, sets his behind upon the floorboards and wags his tail back and forth. I ignore the clicking noise and tell him that his regular walk won't be possible for a little while yet. Scud looks dejected, until I announce that I can throw some sticks for him behind the cottage.

"Nobody will see us," I say, heading for the back door. "It'll be you and me together, Scud. Together for ever more."

Outside, my beagle is in fine form. Despite his hobble, he leaps for the sticks that I throw him and misses none. It almost feels as if he has recovered some of his youth along with his life, for I have not seen him this energetic in a long

time. I also con-
sider it fortunate that he is
still unable to bark. It means we are
free to play for as long as we like without attracting any attention. Scud cannot jump
higher than the fence around our cottage, after all.
Still, I throw my stick up with increasing force, for
there is nothing my dear beagle likes better than
catching it in his jaws before it hits the ground.

I can only blame myself for what happens next. I simply intend to loft it as
high as I can. I do not mean for the
stick to connect with a passing wood
pigeon.

All I can say is that the stick is
not alone in returning to earth.

"Leave it alone!" I cry at Scud,
fearful that he might harm the bird
as it flops to the ground. Even before I have
reached it, however, I am certain the impact
with my stick has proven fatal. The poor
thing gazes up through slack eyes, with one
wing outstretched like an accordion bel-
low and the other folded beneath its body.
"I'm *so* sorry," I say, crouching
before the dead pigeon. "I feel
terrible." Scud must sense my

distress, for he slips beside me and nuzzles my cheek. Before I can stop him, he then licks the bird on the ground. To my relief he does not go on to grab it in his jaws and submits when I grasp his collar to haul him back.

"I suppose you know how it feels to pass away," I say after a moment. Scud makes a pitiful wheezing sound. I believe it is his way of whining. I think to myself that perhaps my dog could excavate his grave once more so we could bury the dead pigeon. As I prepare to collect the bird's corpse in my hands, I am shocked to note the slightest twitch from its outstretched wing. At first I think it must be the breeze, but then it happens again. When the pigeon blinks I just stare, then gasp as it gathers itself, ruffles its feathers and finally takes to the air.

As the bird disappears over the cottage, I wonder if I might have imagined it all. What stops me from scratching my head is the sound of a knock at our front door.

I glance at Scud. He looks at me expectantly, as if he'd like me to throw another stick. "Stay outside," I command him, keeping my voice down low. "And don't go licking any more dead things!"

I open the door to be presented with a casserole dish. Petra Appollonio is behind it. Her head is tipped so I can only see her good side. I feel bad that she feels she must be like this with me. At any other time, I would encourage her to face me directly. All I want now is for her to leave.

"You need to keep up your strength," she says

before I can claim to be busy, and sweeps inside with the pot. "If you'll allow me to reheat it on your stove, I can have it ready for when your father returns from work."

"Thank you," I say, a little lost for words.

"I thought I might dine with you," adds Petra, heading for the kitchen now. "Without Scud for company, this must feel like such a lonely time."

"I feel he is not far away," I reply, cringing to myself.

I follow Petra into the kitchen. She turns to face me directly. This time, it is not the scalding on one side of her face that causes me to avert my gaze.

It is the sight of my dear dog popping into view at the window behind her. With his front paws on the ledge, his remaining eye meets mine and appears to fire up. Scud's tongue is lolling stupidly from the side of his jaw and I know he just wants to say hello to our guest. He seems crestfallen when I glare at him.

"You mustn't blame yourself," observes Petra, who seems a little perplexed when I snap my gaze back at her. "From what the truck driver told me, it happened so suddenly that Scud would have felt little pain. Apparently he went directly under the front wheels and then the back. It would've been over for him in moments."

As she speaks, my reanimated beagle begins

32

bouncing up and down at the glass. He does so with such urgency that a cloud of loose hairs breaks free from his coat, while his ears flap like the wings of a gull. Petra clearly notes a shift in my gaze once more, for this time she turns to see what has drawn my attention.

"Don't look!" I grasp her by the shoulder, bringing her back around. "There is nothing to see but Scud's grave," I say. "I wouldn't wish to upset you unnecessarily."

Petra Appollonio appears a little bit frustrated. It's as if I've denied her the real reason she has paid me this visit. I'd never thought of her as the nosy type, but it is clear from the way her jawline tightens that she is determined to find out what is out there.

"If I might place this dish upon the stove," she says next, and switches around before I can stop her. I see no sign of Scud, however, which is a huge relief as the stove is directly in front of the window. "It won't take long to warm up," she says, upon which my resurrected beagle lifts into view. With his paws upon the sill, Scud seems delighted to see her.

I cannot say that Petra responds in the same way.

5

The first scream from my unexpected guest happens a moment after the casserole dish hits the floor and shatters. This is followed by a short silence as Petra draws breath into her lungs. Then she makes such a fearful racket I fear she may draw attention from the lane.

"Do not be alarmed," I plead, though my dog fails to help matters. Switching from the window to the door, Scud can be heard scraping his claws down the woodwork in a bid to be let in. It doesn't sound good.

Petra makes no attempt to move. She remains rooted to the spot with her palms pressed to her cheeks and her mouth wide open in horror. "What is that?" she asks in a whisper. "What is that *thing*?"

34

"Petra," I say, after some hesitation, "I believe news of Scud's death has been a little premature."

She turns to face me. All the colour from the good side of her face has drained away. "But that was no beagle," she replies fearfully. "There is a *hellhound* at your door!"

Immediately, I realize that my friend does not even recognize the dog. Mindful of the promise I had made to my father to keep Scud's existence a secret, I decide it might be wise to share in her shock.

"If we stay quiet," I suggest, "maybe it will go away."

Together, we face the door once more. Outside, Scud begins to whine. The way his lungs rattle, however, it sounds more like heavy breathing. I trade glances with Petra. She looks absolutely terror-struck. One side of her face has turned the colour of flour. It leaves me feeling bad.

"If I share a secret," I say with some reluctance, "will you promise not to breathe a word?"

"Please don't tell me there is more than one," she replies. "If you do, then I might faint."

I smile uncomfortably. "There's only one Scud."

This time, having gathered her wits a little, Petra Appollonio considers what I have just said. "Lumin, your dog perished under a truck. He suffered *terrible* injuries. The vehicle flattened him."

I look to the floor for a moment. With my hands clasped behind my back, I struggle to find the best way to explain myself.

"He got a bit better," I say eventually, and face her once more. "Would you like to say hello?"

"*No!*" Petra Appollonio blocks my path to the back door and clamps her hands against each side of the frame. She shakes her head furiously at me. "Lumina, that beast is not of this world! What is happening here?"

I sigh to myself, wishing Scud would sound a little less desperate and determined out there. "Do you swear not to tell another living soul? My father's job depends on it."

"He knows about this too?" Petra frowns, sounding less alarmed now.

I nod solemnly. "He is responsible for bringing Scud back from the dead," I say. "Now if you'll be seated, I shall clear up this mess and explain everything."

MEASURE THIS

By the time I have picked up the broken crockery and mopped the floor, Petra Appollonio knows all about Scud's rebirth. She barely blinks when I finish. It is clear she is stunned by what I have shared. I am just not sure she believes a single word. As my dog has continued to scratch and scrape at the door, I suggest there is only one way to prove it.

"Very well," she says with some reluctance and retreats to the other side of the kitchen. "You may let him in, but promise me he will not attempt to rip out my throat."

"Scud is the same as he always was," I insist.

"Apart from the burning red eye and a face like a death mask."

"I mean, you know how friendly he can be!"

38

With Petra braced, I open the door by a crack and command my dog to sit. Then I open up and stand aside.

Petra draws breath to scream, only to clamp a hand across her mouth. Scud remains where he is but wags his tail from side to side.

"You get used to the clicking," I say, feeling ever so slightly embarrassed by the sound. "All he wants to do is greet you properly."

Petra turns her wide eyes to me, drops her hand and nods. "Very well. But if he tries to lick my face I think I will be sick."

I turn to Scud. "In you come, boy."

Despite his disjointed lope, my dog scrabbles eagerly across the tiles. Scud has always been very fond of Petra. Not only does he enjoy romping with her angels on walks, he knows she always keeps her pockets filled with broken biscuit treats. Before he can search them out, however, Petra scatters a handful as if it were garlic in the path of a vampire.

"That's close enough," she mutters as Scud falls upon the offering. Petra observes him for a moment, before crinkling her nose and gagging quietly to herself. "I don't wish to be rude," she says, "but your dog smells as bad as he looks."

With a shrug, I say, "It's my old Scud on the inside. I know that for sure."

By now, my dog has finished wolfing down the

biscuits. He licks his black lips with a tongue that is strikingly blue and then takes himself to his bed in the corner. There, he circles several times before collapsing contentedly in a heap. Within seconds, he is in such a deep sleep that Petra wonders if he has just expired.

"It might be for the best," she says, creeping closer for a better look. "He would at least be at peace." Grimacing to herself, she places a palm upon Scud's chest. On detecting a heartbeat, she frowns and turns to face me. "This isn't natural, Lumina. It looks like you have a corpse in your kitchen."

"It's how he rests nowadays," I say. "He'll surface again within an hour or so. Mark my words."

Petra returns her attention to my slumbering beagle. When she strokes Scud's coat, I begin to think she might be warming to him. "I must say your father has done a remarkable job," she says, and trails a finger alongside one of the many seams that criss-cross Scud's torso. "Apart from the smell, I suppose he really is on the mend."

"I believe the scars will disappear. Scud is healing from the heart, after all."

With a gasp from both Petra and myself, we turn to find my father at the doorway. He eyes Petra warily and then addresses me. "This is supposed to be our secret, Lumina. I cannot afford to lose my job over this."

Petra rises to her feet, adjusting her shawl and smoothing down her skirt as she does so. "What have you done here? Mister Lupesco, this defies the laws of nature."

"And doing nothing would have gone against my duty as a father," he replies. "I have no wish to play God here, Petra. All I care about is my daughter's happiness. Can you not see what this means to her?"

Petra considers me for a moment and then observes my dog once more. "I accept he is no monster on the inside. It is the outside that troubles me though."

"It's the same old Scud," I say. "He's simply had a bigger brush with death than we can imagine."

Petra smiles at this, her expression softening.

"There are no dark arts involved," my father adds. "Scud is rejuvenating thanks to a carefully placed injection of mineral extracts. I swear I cast no spell and made no pact with the devil. For a beagle, he looks a little unsettling, but I have every faith that very soon his health will be fully restored."

When she nods to herself, I do believe our friend is on the way to understanding the fix we're in. "Your secret is safe with me," says Petra. "I know you care about beagles as much as I do, and Scud has always been a very special specimen. This just makes him all the more unique."

I look between Petra and my father. "We can trust her," I say. "She knows how much Scud means to me."

"If I can help in any way," says Petra, "you only have to ask. I confess it has been a shock, but now I am as pleased to see him back with us as you are."

My father weighs up her offer, rasping the bristles on his chin. "Scud needs exercising," he says. "As everyone believes he has died, there is no way Lumina or I can take this beagle out without attracting attention."

"I could walk him," she offers, which appears to be just what my father was hoping she would say. "Scud can join my pack of angels tomorrow morning. Everyone knows I rescue beagles. Should anyone ask, I will simply say that he is a new addition to my heavenly host."

Petra's puppies = angles from above
Angles?
Angels!
Angels!
Angels!
Angels!
Angels!
Angels!
Angels!
ANGELS!

6

Throughout his life, up until the accident, Scud's health and welfare had been my responsibility.

I didn't just feed him twice a day and keep his water bowl brimming. I administered a monthly worming pill and an ointment to guard him against ticks. Like most dogs, Scud would wriggle as I struggled to slot the pill down his throat, while an application of the ointment would see him sulk right up until his next meal. Despite this, I like to think he knew that I was acting in his best interest. Not once did he fall sick or pick up an infestation and bring it into the house.

I understand that Scud's collision with a truck really knocked the stuffing from him. I appreciate that in this recovery period his immune system might be somewhat fragile. In such a state, I would not have been surprised if he found it hard to fight off fleas. What I could not have anticipated was that the poor thing would become plagued by *flies*.

"What can we do?" I ask my father the next morning.

Before us, Scud lies dejectedly with his head on his front paws. His eye is still glowing red, but that's the only spark in him. Every now and then he twitches one ear or the other. It does little to drive away the swarm. I count at least a dozen, all of them swooping and looping around my poor beagle.

"Have you tried the flea powder?" my father asks.

I tell him I have used up half a bottle and even resorted to swatting at them with a newspaper. "They are just too quick," I say. "Petra will be here at any moment. We cannot send him out in this condition."

My father sighs to himself. "Check under the sink," he says. "Behind the bleach you'll find a canister of fly spray."

I face him side-on, surprised by the suggestion. "Is that stuff suitable for using on pets?"

Before he can answer, Scud rises up and scratches furiously at himself with his good hindleg. Then he switches to the opposite side and promptly loses his balance.

"Put it this way, Lumin: it can't kill him. You might even find it masks the smell."

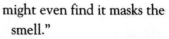

46

❦   ❦   ❦

By the time Petra knocks at the door to collect my dog, I have dealt with all but two of the flies. They continue to circle the crown of his head like crows around a steeple, but there is nothing more that I can do. Having used up all the fly spray, I had set about them with the swatter.

At that point Scud became quite spooked. I assured him I was not attempting to strike him. Even so, I felt guilty when he cowed from me and gave him a cuddle instead.

"With luck, they'll buzz away once he's outside." My father grasps the handle to open the door. "He could certainly benefit from a breath of fresh air."

I slip Scud's lead around his neck. He always gets excited at the prospect of a walk. On hearing Petra greet my father, he perks up notably.

"My angels are so looking forward to seeing their old friend," she says. "Is Scud ready?"

"He certainly is." My father stands aside so she may see us. Petra has brought half a dozen beagles with her. They sit obediently at her feet. Until, that is, my dog bounds out to join them. I am as startled as Petra when every single one turns tail in fright. She has each of them on a lead, of course, but her yelping angels are so desperate to get away that they drag her around on the spot.

47

"Calm," she yells over the din, and grabs the leads with both hands. *"Calm!"*

Despite such a disorderly outbreak, Petra is an accomplished dog handler. At once, but clearly with some reluctance, her beagles fall quiet. I know that Scud's appearance has startled them and apologize to Petra. "He can't help it," I say, by way of explanation.

"I'm sure your dogs will settle once they realize he means no harm," my father adds.

Petra calms the last of her angels. Having collected herself, but still looking a little tense, she offers us both a brave smile. "We'll consider it an adventure," she says, and gestures for me to pass her Scud's lead. "You can be sure he won't misbehave with me."

As soon as Petra has possession of Scud, she arranges her angels so that he is in the middle of the pack. The other dogs do as they're told, but it is clear to my father and me that if they had the chance they would flee for the hills.

"I am sorry about the fly infestation," I say, on noting the increase in activity around Scud's head and body. "I don't think it's something your angels can catch."

Petra pretends not to notice. Instead, she gathers all the leads in one hand before promising to return within the hour.

Angels
— NOT angles —

48

"Just don't let him run free," my father calls out as she reaches the gate. "We need him back in one piece."

Together, we watch Petra make her way down the street. Scud may move very differently from his fellow beagles, but in such a number he does not stand out as I had feared. Indeed, Petra even passes two old ladies on their way back from market who greet her without a second glance.

"Petra is a kind soul," my father says, before turning to prepare for work. "Without her, the beagles around here would be running wild."

Everyone knows that this town is home to an unusual number of the same dog breed. We just do not like to talk openly about the reason why. It is no secret that the spa employs beagles to ensure its products meet the highest standards. According to the scientific community, their medium size and passive nature makes them perfect for their needs. They are caged within the lab complex, where the scientists use them to check the safety of the shampoos and scrubs, the conditioners, balms and body oils. Testing spa products on these dogs divides opinion. Many people side with Doctor Grubo. He believes most fiercely that it is the surest way to check that a new product won't cause allergies, adverse reactions, strange side-effects or anything that could harm human health. Personally, I believe there has to be another way. So, too, does my father. But as Doctor Grubo simply fires or retires any employee who voices a concern, he has adopted a more subtle approach.

This is also the reason why my father cannot afford to lose his job. He could find work elsewhere, of course, but without his presence in the lab those poor beagles would have no hope of a better life.

Nor would it be possible for me to assist him.

"I plan to visit the lagoon today," I say, on handing my father his sandwiches. "Are you testing today?"

"I am indeed." He beams. "And you'd be more than welcome to help me out."

We exchange a goodbye kiss on the cheek.

"If there is anything I can do," I reply, "you only have to ask."

7

One hour after Petra left to walk the dogs, I begin to worry. Alone in the cottage, I wonder whether perhaps my dog has bolted once again.

Scud only has to get a whiff of deer or hare and his chase instinct takes over. If he made a break without warning, Petra would have stood little chance of holding on to him. I am fretting about this at the window when she appears at the front gate. Her angels flock around her, and I know that Scud is among them on account of all the flies.

"Thank you so much," I say on opening the door. At once, Scud does exactly as I had feared. He breaks from the pack, trailing his lead and the little black swarm behind him, which is a relief when I

crouch to greet him. He is panting heavily. Every breath causes his lungs to squeak and whistle.

"For a dog back from the dead, he certainly has a lust for life." Petra looks a little puffed. I draw breath to ask her if Scud has behaved himself, only for her to assure me that the experience was a pleasure. "My angels ensured he attracted no attention, but I can't say the same for the flies." She pauses there to bat at the swarm. "This infestation has certainly swelled since we set off. If you can find a way to deal with the problem, I will be happy to walk Scud any time you like."

As she speaks, an exhausted Scud leaves me for his bed. We watch him turning circles before dropping down as if somehow all the bones have vanished from his legs.

"You don't have to worry about the flies," I assure her. "There is one other way of dealing with them that I have yet to try."

I arrive at the spa in good spirits. Not only is my dear dog back with me, slumbering happily now we have found a way to exercise him undercover, I believe I am in control of the infestation. All I had done was fashion a collar from strips of sticky flypaper. Scud was so lifeless that he didn't even blink when I fixed it around his neck, where it began to work straight away. I realize I will have to change it regularly on account of the accumulation of little black corpses. What pleases me is that I feel able to cater for Scud's new needs.

"I have my membership card," I tell the receptionist, but she just smiles and waves me in.

As I make my way towards the changing rooms, I pass a door that has been left ajar. Normally, I would walk on by, but the groaning from within causes me to falter. At first I think that someone must be injured in there. Concerned, I take a peek and realize I am looking in upon the massage room.

"Will you please stop wriggling!" complains Gertruda Gašper. On the padded table before her, Doctor Grubo is lying on his stomach with only a

towel around his waist. There is a hole at one end of the table, through which the spa owner has placed his face. Judging by his expression, it is clear he is in some degree of pain. His eyes are bulging and his teeth gritted tight. I am not surprised at all, for Gertruda is pressing down between his shoulder blades using the knuckles of her clasped hands. She is doing so with all her might, which is clearly quite considerable.

"I have a strained trapezius muscle, Gertruda. We are not in the torture business here."

"Oh, stop fussing. It is the price you pay for not warming up properly before you exercise. When will you learn? There is a procedure to follow when it comes to working out. You cannot simply begin pumping iron without risk of injury. Your performance medication does not make you invincible, after all."

Doctor Grubo opens his mouth to reply, only to exhale with a grunt as the masseuse pushes the breath from his lungs. "Go gently for pity's sake!" he bellows through the hole. This time, I see what is visible of his face contort and turn a furious red. It is quite unreal, like nothing I have ever seen before, and cannot be natural. Both of his eyes suddenly look like painted Ping-Pong balls preparing to pop on to the floor. I shrink from the door in alarm. I am also surprised that Gertruda Gašper maintains both calm and control. I would rather be in that room with a hungry tiger than the spa director looking this enraged. Instead of releasing her hold and backing away to give him space, the masseuse simply pushes down harder. It almost appears as if she has trapped him there, which is perhaps the best way of handling the man when he's in a mood.

"Don't be a baby," she tells him, and executes an almighty shove between his shoulder blades.

"I'm almost done. You'll thank me for it when I'm finished."

Her promise is marked by a sickening crunch. For a moment, I fear she has broken his back. Doctor Grubo roars at the top of his voice and then falls quite still. Gertruda steps away now, brushing her palms as if to mark a job well done. Next, I see him open his eyes. He blinks several times and then smiles broadly at the floor.

"You've done it," he says, and lifts his face from the hole in the table. "I feel as good as new! Gertruda, I could hug you!"

"That won't be necessary," she says. "Sometimes I think you don't know your own strength."

Doctor Grubo swings from the table and onto his feet. Transfixed, I continue to spy through the crack in the door.

"I don't know what I would do without you," he tells her, climbing back into his shirt. "You're a credit to my clinic."

"You can always trust me to restore order," replies Gertruda modestly.

"Indeed I can." Having buttoned himself up, Doctor Grubo produces a bow tie from his pocket. He begins to tie it around his collar, only for the masseuse to take over. "You and I make a good team," he tells her, with his chin tipped high so she can finish the job. "I can always rely on you to ensure that people obey the rules. And if they don't, you only have to say the word and I will *crush* them!"

The way he says this, with such inner fury, causes me to gasp. At once, Doctor Grubo turns his head in my direction. I shrink away and cross my fingers as I hurry along the corridor in the hope that he did not see me.

The sun plays tricks on me today. A clear blue sky reaches overhead and, though the sun seems distant, it is shining brightly. Still, when I step out from the changing rooms in my costume and swim cap, the brisk temperature takes my breath away.

The experience is unpleasant, but in some ways it makes the plunge into the steaming thermal waters of the lagoon all the more enjoyable. My toes sink through the silt floor as I make my way into the middle. There, with my eyes tightly shut and a smile upon my face, I float upon my back in the shadow of the power station

and simply relax. Any worries I might've had that Doctor Grubo had caught me eavesdropping simply wash away. Sometimes I think this is how it must feel to be in the womb. All sense of the outside world stops at the lagoon's rocky edges. Indeed, by the time I climb out to shower and dress, it feels as if I have been born again. It means when I find my father with the beagles, testing products in the lab, I am ready to give him all the help he needs.

"Lumina, you've arrived at the right moment." My father is drawing an oily, greenish liquid from a tube using a little glass dropper. He's at the bench in the testing room, working under a strip light. In a pen behind him I count six young beagles in total. They watch him dolefully. "Perhaps you can help me with this."

"What is it?" I ask.

My father examines the dropper under the light. I glance at the beagles. They're watching his every move.

"A new body oil I've been working on. Everything has tested fine. All I have to do is make sure it won't sting the eyes." He invites me to take the dropper. "Would you do the honours, Lumin?"

I step around the bench, with my back to the dogs, and take the dropper. I hear them whimpering behind me when I squeeze a little from the tip to check it is not blocked. My father then tips his

60

head up to the light and gently draws down one lower eyelid with his fingertips. "Go ahead, my girl. I'm ready."

When my father first elected to test all products on himself, I worried about his wellbeing. *"What if you hurt yourself?"* I asked. *"You could be scarred, burned, blinded!"* His response was very simple. *"So, too, could the dogs, Lumina, and I am not prepared to make them suffer."*

Luckily, my father's skills as a scientist mean he has yet to test anything that has caused him serious harm. Once, he returned home with his chest covered in hives. The hair-removal cream responsible was later abandoned, as was the foot balm that upset his stomach for a week after he swallowed it. I did question why anyone would think to taste a product intended for tired toes. My father just shrugged and reminded me that

61

sometimes people behaved in ways we could not understand. Doctor Grubo's belief that beagles were good for nothing but testing products certainly confounded us.

When he first introduced the system, my father had protested in the strongest terms. The doctor did not listen. He simply informed my father that if he didn't like it, he could work elsewhere. My father would've gone, but then the first consignment of puppies arrived. As soon as he opened up the box and saw all those big brown eyes peering up at him, he knew he had to stay. From that moment on, my father pledged to do everything he could to free them by working from the inside.

"How does that feel?" I ask, watching my father blinking rapidly.

"Like I've got a drop of body oil in my eye," he says. "It stings a bit, but if I dilute the mixture a little it'll be perfectly safe."

I hand him a box of tissues before turning my attention to the beagles. "How are we today?" I ask, crouching at the pen. "If only you knew what a lucky break you've had here."

The dogs respond by crowding for my attention. I slip a hand through the bar to pet them all and then find my father at my side.

"Aren't they beautiful?" he says, still dabbing at his eye. "I remember when Scud first arrived here. I

62

knew he would make a great friend for you, and I wasn't wrong."

Smiling, I continue to stroke and pat the beagles. "Which one of these will be next to fall sick?"

"The unhappiest," my father replies quite frankly. "I only wish Doctor Grubo wouldn't be so quick to replace them."

Scud was the first beagle that my father sprung from the lab. A dog must be in full health to provide accurate test results, which is how he came to be released. My father pretended poor Scud was asthmatic. When Doctor Grubo ordered the dog's destruction, my

father simply offered to rehouse him. I do not like to think about the consequences should the spa director ever discover the truth. We both know how hot-headed he can be. If he knew how he was being fooled, I fear he would explode into violence. Without a doubt, this makes my father a very brave man indeed. Despite the risk of injury, he continues to liberate beagles housed here for testing. Every now and then, he registers a dog as sick, lame or injured and then takes it away at the end of the day. There is nothing wrong with any of them, of course, but Doctor Grubo is unaware of that. Frankly, he doesn't even care about their welfare. The fact that my father takes each beagle straight to the door of Petra Appollonio is of no interest to him. Doctor Grubo's only concern is that the local puppy farm can deliver swiftly in order to make up the numbers.

"That one looks sad." I point at the smallest beagle at the back and then look appealingly at my father. "Petra would give it all the love in the world."

My father knows what I am hinting at here. I am always picking out the beagle in most need of affection, and when he sighs and nods his head I know he has just agreed.

"But first let me place an order with the puppy farm," he says, and rises to his feet. "As much as I hate requesting another new beagle for the lab, at least I know they will come to no harm here."

"I think of it as a halfway house," I say: "the last stop before true freedom."

On my way out of the spa, following the corridor overlooking the lagoon, my thoughts return to Scud. I feel sure that he will not have stirred. My main concern is how many flies I might find stuck to his new collar.

"Lumina! No doubt a session in our healing waters will have helped to ease your grief."

I've just passed an open door when the voice calls out to me. I halt in my tracks and take a step back.

"Doctor Grubo," I say, on finding the man himself beaming at me from behind his desk. The walls in here are decorated with framed pictures from his

career as a bodybuilder. I even see an old sepia portrait of him receiving a medal from our president. He invites me to come inside and be seated. I have a choice between a rowing machine on the floor beside his desk or a chair in front of it. I assume he means the latter. Nervously, I do as I am told. As I settle myself into the chair, I note one of the desk drawers is open. The doctor shuts it smartly, but not before I have caught a glimpse of several medicine bottles in there. I jump in my seat and look back at him.

"How are you feeling now?" he asks, and tips his head to one side. All the time, his pool-blue eyes stay locked on me.

If he is aware that I eavesdropped on his session in the massage room, he does not appear to show it. Either Doctor Grubo is a very good actor, or I had a lucky escape.

"I enjoyed a pleasant swim," I say, mindful not to steer on to the subject of dogs. "It certainly lifted my spirits."

Naturally, Doctor Grubo is unaware that after my regular session in the lagoon I often steal into the lab to pet the beagles. As far as he is concerned, those dogs are working animals until such a time arises when they are unfit for the job. Even though

67

I am always careful to slip in undetected, I find him appraising me with what looks increasingly like an air of suspicion. I really don't wish to upset him. All I can do is smile hesitantly. It comes as a relief when that serves to draw him from his thoughts.

"I must say you look radiant, little Lumin, for a girl in mourning. I have no doubt that you'll bounce back very quickly indeed."

"I hope so," I say, and fidget uncomfortably as he leans forward upon his forearms.

"A word of advice," he says: "you would do well to develop an interest now in something that cannot die on you. As a small boy, on losing my poor python, I swore I would never place myself in such a vulnerable position again. Do you know what I did instead?" he asks, but gives no time for me to even guess. "I devoted all my care and attention to the upkeep of my body."

"Oh," I say, a little startled when he rises from his chair and then curls his arm at the elbow. Clenching his teeth and fist before me, I watch in awe as his muscles inflate inside his shirtsleeves. I even see a branch of veins swelling up through the white cotton fabric. "It's clear you're still committed to the cause," I add. "For a man of your age, you must be very proud."

Doctor Grubo seems somewhat crestfallen all of a sudden. "At my age?" he repeats, and relaxes his arm. "Young lady, at my age I am in *peak* physical condition! Must I prove myself?"

"No! Of course not—"

"Stand aside!"

I am not just startled by this unexpected outburst but by the fact that he goes on to vault over the desk using one hand as a spring.

"There really is no need," I say, having retreated to the door.

"Yes, there is!" he snaps, so forcefully my stomach knots.

Without another word, Doctor Grubo drops to the floor. There, he begins to perform a series of push-ups. I think he might stop at ten, and then twenty. By the time he reaches fifty, I dare to suggest he has proved his point.

"I am impressed," I say, as he continues to call out each number. "I am sure men half your age could not manage such a feat."

Doctor Grubo does not appear to hear me. He seems totally driven, despite the effort involved. All I can do is watch in silence and remind myself not to ask where he gets his strength from.

On completing one hundred push-ups, the spa director pauses to gather his breath before squat-jumping back to his feet.

"There," he says, his face glossy with sweat. "Nothing like a little exercise to get the heart pumping."

The way he looks, I am surprised it has not burst clean through his ribcage. I really would like to make my excuses and leave. My worry is that after such a display it might offend him, and I don't wish to provoke him again. So, instead, I say, "You're certainly passionate about staying in good shape."

"It's a passion for *life*," he says, and returns to his seat. "Far be it from me to tell you how to lead yours, Lumin, but perhaps now is your chance to break free from the tyranny of caring for a pet. Look after your body instead. OK, so it needs regular exercise, food and water, plus a warm place to sleep at night, but it won't run away and get into mortal mischief. Do you understand what I'm saying here?"

There is no way I can tell Doctor Grubo about Scud. At the same time, I am left wondering why he has shown such interest in my welfare. "I do understand," I say finally, "but I don't think I have the passion to become a bodybuilder."

Doctor Grubo looks baffled by my response. Then he chuckles to himself. At first it looks like he'll quickly recover his composure. Instead, his amusement grows so much I have no choice but to laugh along with him.

"Dear girl," he says, "there's only room for one bodybuilding legend in this spa town. Of *course* I am not suggesting you sculpt your sinews to perfection! I am simply encouraging you to find an interest in life that does not have four legs and a tail." At this, with his eyes still on me, Doctor Grubo's smile fades. "Attachment to a dog can only end in tears, Lumina. Mark my words."

All the way home, I reflect on Doctor Grubo's advice. I cannot believe that the secret about Scud is out. Even so, his little chat had been most strange indeed. In order to avoid panicking about it, I remind myself that if he was wise to exactly who

71

was behind my dog's resurrection then my father would've been sacked on the spot.

As I follow the lane home, crossing over at times to avoid any steaming cracks, I decide that time spent with Scud will help to ease my anxieties. Since my beagle came back to me, simply being in his company has made everything feel fine. I know we face difficulties in keeping his existence undercover. I am also aware that the stink through his skin and the issue with the flies make him less appealing as a dog I would like curled up at my feet. Even so, when we are together, nothing else matters in the whole wide world.

Which would explain my sheer panic when I arrive home to find that he has gone.

"Scud?" Having searched every room I decide to look outside. As soon as I arrive at the back door, my worst fears come true. Not only is it unlocked, I realize it has also been left open. Immediately, I rush outside to call for him. I am forced to do so without shouting, however. Despite the seriousness of the situation, I cannot be seen to be appealing for a dog to return who is supposedly six feet under. "*Scud*, where are you?"

I wheel around in desperation, seeking out some trail he might've left, and find just such a thing. Long before the accident, Scud had liked to head off on adventures by himself. He would never cause any harm and had always returned safely, apart from that fateful day when he crossed in the path of a truck.

When I spot evidence of burrowing under the fence, I feel sure my beagle's old habits are another thing that has not died.

10

Within minutes, I am out scouring the lanes.
Before appealing for Scud to return, I glance over
my shoulder to be sure that I am not within earshot.
This proves to be difficult as I approach the main
square. It's market day, and people are out in great
numbers. With stalls arranged around the
great geyser and traders bawling out their
wares, it is hard for me to search for him
without attracting some attention. I still
call his name but
wait for the
regular erup-
tion of steam
for cover. This

74

is a likely area for
me to be looking. On
several escape bids in the past,
I have found my beagle sniffing around
the fish and meat counters. Once he
managed to snatch a sirloin steak. Which
is why I make every effort not to catch the
butcher's eye.

"Lumina? You look worried."

I turn, on hearing my name, to find Petra
queuing for dried fruit. She is without her
angels and is, instead, carrying a wicker bas-
ket in the crook of her arm. She also wears a
shawl over her head, which I know she uses
to pinch across her face at times when people
make her feel uncomfortable.

"I have lost something special," I say, and
pull a face in the hope that she'll know
what I mean. "Not for the first time
either."

Petra tips her head, seemingly mystified. When she realizes that I must be talking about Scud, she leaves the queue immediately. "But we left him dead to the world, Lumina. He was sleeping so deeply I didn't think he'd wake again for another hundred years!"

"He has vanished," I say plainly. "I found the door ajar and a hole burrowed under the fence. Petra, I fear Scud must be up to his old tricks."

Petra thinks about this for a moment. "I suppose we can be assured that he has not been spotted yet," she tells me. "Otherwise, all hell would have broken loose."

I draw breath to agree, only for a shriek to sail over the square.

At once, all eyes turn to the lane winding out towards the clinic and the power station. There is nothing to see at first. Then two young women come rushing into view. They are both clearly scared witless. When one looks over her shoulder, I fear that I may see Scud bounding after them in the belief that they're playing a game. When that doesn't happen, I turn to Petra and question what is happening here.

"I think we should hurry," she replies, and draws my attention to the fact that many people are now moving towards the two terror-stricken girls. "If Scud really is behind this then your beagle might

76

well find himself facing a mob."

Together, we take off towards the stricken pair.

"*What has happened?*" I hear someone call.

"Something horrible!" one cries, and falls into the arms of the first man to reach her.

"Something hideous!" her friend chimes in, who promptly sinks to her knees.

I glance at Petra, feeling my own legs weakening. "I think I might have some explaining to do," I say quietly, only to fall silent when the first girl speaks again.

"A *badger*!" she says breathlessly. "The badger that's been rotting at the side of the lane for the last week…"

"The road kill?" asks the man, still clutching her. "What about it?"

This time, Petra and I share the same baffled glance at one another. It is not uncommon around here to see wildlife that has met a sorry end on account of the traffic to and from the power station and the spa. Scud was the first domestic pet I have known to have been knocked down by a truck. Generally, it was creatures from the woodlands and the lower slopes of the mountains that tended to wander onto the cobbles and freeze in the headlamps. Badgers were not uncommon, nor hares and sometimes deer, so I cannot understand why the sight of one such corpse could have caused

77

this degree of upset. If they weren't cleared away by a good Samaritan in the shape of a passing motorist or pedestrian, eventually another animal in the food chain would creep out and claim them for their supper. Everyone knows this, which is why a hush descends as the young woman prepares to explain herself.

"We were passing by when the badger's tail twitched!" she begins. "We believed our eyes were deceiving us, but then the creature's back legs flexed and it began to peel itself from the stones."

At this, some people in the crowd gasp out loud. Others express their disbelief. But all continue to listen with bated breath.

"Right before us," her friend adds hurriedly. "I swear I saw its flattened torso pop into shape. Even its bones could be heard clicking back into position."

"The worst part was when it raised its snout and looked at us," the first girl goes on. "I have never seen such demonic eyes! Like red-hot coals, I swear!"

"And the *smell*," her friend stresses. "I know we are used to sulphurous gases rising up from the earth, but when mixed with rotten flesh…" She trails away there, and her focus falls slack. I notice people looking at one another, wondering how to react.

"Where is this creature now?" someone asks.

The two girls look at one another. "When I screamed," answers the first to speak, "it took off into the undergrowth."

"You have to believe us," her friend appeals. "There is a *zombie* badger on the loose!"

The gasp from the crowd is echoed by the geyser erupting behind us. My mind is spinning from what we've just heard. Fortunately, Petra Appollonio has the presence of mind to draw me from the crowd before letting me speak.

"Scud is behind this," I tell her. "I have an awful feeling that I know what's happened."

11

On hearing about the badger, my thoughts turn to the poor pigeon that had picked itself up at my feet. At the time, I'd sworn the bird had been struck dead accidentally when my stick had brought it down to earth. When it had seemingly come back to life, I'd simply thought that I had misjudged the severity of the situation. What I had not considered was the fact that Scud had shown an interest in it. My dog had merely slurped its tongue across the bird's feathered chest. Somehow, that had been enough to bring it back from the dead.

"We must find my beagle," I whisper urgently, having shared this episode with Petra. "It is not safe for him to be on the loose!"

By now, some people have broken from the crowd and set off along the lane to investigate. I do not believe that we will find Scud there. Once he has embarked upon an adventure, he doesn't tend to stay in one place for long.

"Where shall we look?" asks Petra, clearly sharing my anxiety. "We know it's Scud on the inside, but if they find him now, looking as he does, they'll set upon him for sure."

My mind races through all the places he might be. The lane leading out to the spa and the power station is flanked on one side by a bank of lava rock, and on the other by a slope of undergrowth. Then I consider the fact that the slope overlooks the church and the graveyard that surrounds it.

"Oh no!" I say to myself, and grab Petra by the wrist. "You know how my dog likes to dig!"

"Do you think he might be looking for bones?" she asks.

"I hope with all my heart that he isn't," I reply, before turning for the church lane.

The graveyard is located in one of the few cool spots within the spa town. Here, the ground does not crack open at random. No steam can be seen rising up among the gravestones. It simply forms a curtain around the perimeter. This is because beneath the

81

soil where the coffins lie is a bed of rock so thick that it serves as a shield to the subterranean heat. According to the local history books, it made sense to build the church here so the dead could be laid to rest without risk of being stewed.

"Do you see him?" Petra follows me through the steam boundary and stops to look around.

"Scud!" I call, hoping I am no longer in earshot. "Scud!"

We begin to walk among the stones, each of us taking a different path. My mother is buried here, but this is not the time to pay my respects. Even so, I find myself following a familiar path around the church, towards the far side where her grave lies.

"He isn't here, Lumin ... no, wait!"

I spin around. Petra's attention is locked on a point towards the slope. When she calls my dog's name and begins to move towards it, I race in the same direction. A moment later, my friend stops in her tracks.

When a clod of soil flops over one of the gravestones ahead of her, I also come to a sudden standstill.

"Oh no," I say to myself when a second volley sprays over the stone. "Scud, stop!"

As soon as I set eyes upon my beagle and his single red orb glows back at me, he knows that he is in trouble. Immediately, he hauls himself out of the hole he has begun, but it's too late for him to

82

pretend he isn't responsible. What troubles me most is that it isn't his first excavation.

"Oh, Scud!" Scandalized, I look around with Petra now. "What have you done?"

"It's like a rabbit warren," my friend remarks. "A warren without the rabbits."

I try to count the number of holes that my dog has begun but quickly give up. I am more concerned by what Scud might have uncovered.

"This is a place of rest," I observe. "What has he disturbed here?"

Petra peers into several holes. "Heaven help us if he's reached any coffins. I have no desire to meet my ancestors!"

I turn my attention to Scud. "We need to get you home," I say, and note how my improvised collar around his neck has become thickened by black spots. At the same time, I see several flies buzzing around his head. "And not just to freshen you up."

I have brought his lead with me, which I quickly clip to his real collar underneath all that sticky tape. It isn't pleasant, but then Scud is my dog and I am a responsible owner.

"Somehow we need to get him out of here without being spotted." Petra turns her attention to the road beyond the slope. It is hard to see much on account of the steam, but clearly a crowd has gathered at the site where the badger had come back to life. "People are on the lookout for something demonic," she adds, glancing at the one dog that couldn't look less terrifying if he tried. "I will have to fetch my angels. They can provide the cover Scud needs, but you must stay out of sight with him until I return."

"Petra," I call as she turns to leave, which causes her to come around full circle, "you're very sweet."

Petra smiles, looking uncomfortable at my compliment. At the same time it's clear that the party up on the lane are beginning to widen their search for the badger.

"I suggest you take Scud inside the church," she says, keeping her voice low. "Wait for me there. I will return with my angels as swiftly as I can."

12

From the number of dwellings clustered around the main square, you would think our church ought to be a little bigger. In truth, once you dip your head to get through the door, you find something more suited to a village community. There are six rows of pews in total, and yet this proves more than enough. For when it comes to a place of worship, the great majority have always congregated within the sacred waters of the lagoon.

"This is no time to explore," I tell Scud, who is straining at the lead to look around. I haul my dog towards the pew at the back, and settle there in the shadows. He lies at my feet looking dejected all of a sudden. "What's happening, boy? It's as if the devil has got inside you!"

In response, my beagle rolls onto his back and gazes at me stupidly. With his paws curled, I know he wants me to tickle his tummy and pretend all this is a game. I am just not in the mood. For one thing, it looks like he is impersonating a corpse, which seems a little distasteful at this moment in time. More importantly, I do not wish to disturb the stitching. Even so, I realize Petra was quite right in her observation. For Scud's scars are looking set to heal up perfectly.

"Stop messing around," I say under my breath, and swat at a fly that makes a low pass over his belly. I lean down to pick at a section of his coat under the neck. His time underground, with no life inside him, has left it matted and a little greasy. I have noticed strands shedding in the breeze. What I have not seen, until now, is that a fine regrowth is appearing underneath. I investigate further, only for a clump of old hair to come away completely. "This is quite a moult," I say to myself. "A good brushing would work wonders!"

Before I can groom him with my fingers, my attention is seized by the sound of the church door creaking open. As soon as I realize that it is not Petra Appollonio who has just entered, I duck as low down as I can.

"*Lumina?*"

Unfortunately, it seems my presence has not gone unnoticed. I sit up straight and struggle to appear pleasantly surprised to see Gertruda Gašper.

"I am alone!" I declare, somewhat panicked. Immediately, I grimace at my response. "What I mean to say is that I am alone with my thoughts."

Keen to see Gertruda for himself, Scud makes an attempt to rise. I force him down with my feet and hands. It sounds as if I have just trodden on a packet of crisps. All I can do is smile innocently at the clinic's stern masseuse, while struggling to keep my beagle still, and ask what brings her here.

"I would ask you the same question," she says instead, as I bat away a fly. "Only I believe we *both* know what you're doing."

"Do we?" I glance at Scud. By now, he has resigned himself to lying quietly under my feet.

"Your beagle dog," says Gertruda, and unwinds the shawl she had been wearing over her head. "You are here to grieve the passing of your dog. Am I right?"

"Oh," I say, a little surprised, and shuffle

uncomfortably in my pew. "Yes, I am! That's right. Poor Scud."

Gertruda seems less than sympathetic. I even sense that she is irritated to find me here. It's pretty clear she is still cross about the fact that Doctor Grubo had allowed me to deliver sandwiches to my father. It wasn't a big rule that I had broken, I think to myself. Especially not when I consider the fact that I am currently hiding a dog inside this church that has defied the laws of *creation*.

With this in mind, I make sure my feet are firmly planted on my poor beagle and pretend to wipe away a tear. Gertruda regards me for a moment more than is comfortable.

"You need to toughen up in the face of tragedy," she says eventually. "When my cottage collapsed, I did not crumble with it. Look on the bright side, child. We all know a dog is for life, but if it passes away prematurely you can always get another one. I have no doubt that if you appeal to your father he will place an order for a replacement with the puppy farm."

I am unsurprised by Gertruda's insensitivity. Everyone knows that the loss of her cottage left her with little sense of charity for anyone other than herself. Even so, I am stung by her remarks.

"Scud was one of a kind," I tell her, still pressing down hard on the beagle at my feet. I hear him whimper, and cover it up with a cough.

Increasingly, Gertruda looks like someone who's just sipped from a cup of nettle tea and received a nasty sting. "A beagle is a beagle," she states, quite simply. "I'm sure the puppy farm can cater for your needs."

With that, Gertruda makes her way to the front pew, as far from me as she can possibly be.

The moment that she turns, I breathe out and close my eyes. I had not expected anyone to find me here, after all. Nor did I think that my beagle might seize the opportunity now to wriggle free from under my feet.

"Scud!" I yell, failing to grab his collar as he makes a break for the main entrance. "No, Scud! *No!*"

Even though my beagle's paws slip and scrabble on the stone floor, he is through the open door in a heartbeat. I am up on my feet but abandon the chase as soon as I see Gertruda. She seems as startled as I am. Judging by the way she is looking at me, however, she had not turned in time to be wise to what just happened.

"Lumina, we do not cry over spilt milk and, frankly, your dog is no different. I am sure he's watching over you at this very moment."

"I doubt that somehow," I mutter, thinking that at this very moment my beagle will be tearing across the cemetery.

"Rest assured, he's in a better place," she replies.

I plant my palm across my forehead, in despair at my dog's disappearance. As I do so, I realize that I must play up to her suspicions if I am to escape from this fix I'm in.

"I cannot believe he has gone!" I wail, as convincingly as I can. "My poor dog is no more!"

Gertruda Gašper sighs huffily, clearly upset by the scene I am creating. "Worse things have happened," she tells me. "Especially to *me*."

I feel desperately uncomfortable, but now I have started this charade it would look even more suspicious if I just stopped abruptly. I look at the masseuse, thinking only about my dog on the loose, and dab at my eyes. "I should leave you in peace," I say, and move towards the door. "Perhaps I need some fresh air."

"Indeed you do," she replies. "Your emotions are quite unruly." Gertruda watches me as I cross the aisle to leave. Once again, her gaze narrows. I know that I am behaving out of character and wonder how much further I can go to keep Scud under wraps. As much as I love my beagle, he has become more trouble back from the dead than alive. At the church door, just as I think I am free to go in search of Scud, Gertruda leaves me with a warning that causes me to falter. "The town is abuzz with word of a strange sighting," she says. "If you see a badger on

91

the loose, seemingly risen from the roadside, you would be wise to steer well clear."

"I am sure such a creature would mean no harm," I call back.

When Gertruda Gašper does not reply, I feel obliged to turn and face her. What she has to say leaves me desperate to track down Scud and stop him from unearthing anything more.

"Mark my words," she says gravely from her pew, "should any such demon cross my path, I shall kill it with my bare hands. There is no space in this spa town for disorder, as we all know."

13

Outside, across the church grounds, I find a crowd has gathered at the spot where I first found Scud. My heart starts to hammer. I cannot see what they have encircled and worry that it might be my dog. My first thought is to run and hide away inside my cottage. Then I consider my canine duty.

I feel dizzy as I approach. But when I realize that they are peering at the holes not the badly behaved beagle who created them, my tension eases.

"If this is the work of the abominable badger," I hear someone mutter, *"we must hunt it down immediately!"*

"The fiend is clearly desperate to dig up the dead, but I have no doubt it will be back. Badgers come out at night, after all."

I stand behind the crowd as the debate continues. When someone asks for volunteers to patrol the spa town after dark, I decide it might be best if I didn't get involved.

I head away before I am noticed and scour the graveyard for any other sign of life or even death. It is only when I decide to check beyond the main gates that I find what I am looking for.

"*Scud!*" I keep my voice low, unwilling to be overheard. Still, it is urgent enough for my dog to pause and peer back at me.

He had been happily wagging what is left of his tail. That falls still when he sees how vexed I am. Had I not spotted him, just as he reached the crest of the lane leading back into town, I fear he would've been met by a less than welcoming party. His appearance is guaranteed to cause outrage. Looking at him now, it's the object in his jaws that would prevent anyone from accepting that he's really not as bad as he looks.

"Put it down, boy. Put it down *now*!"

Scud faces me directly, his one red eye burning defiantly, and shakes his head from side to side. The flies are back in force and he has left a stink in his wake that by rights should be enough to wake the dead.

My main concern, however, is the big thigh bone

I have caught him carrying away. "You *know* that doesn't belong to you," I scold him. "Now be a good boy and do as I ask."

My beagle does nothing of the sort. As I approach, he retreats in such a way that I realize he has misunderstood me.

"This isn't a game!" I wail, and yet every time I lunge for my dog, he simply ducks away playfully. I am so tense and frustrated that I think I might cry. I'm also slightly frightened at what might come hopping from the graveyard at any moment. It's only when a voice commands Scud to be still and sit that my spirits lift.

"*Petra!*" I declare, as my dog obeys the instruction at once. "Thank goodness you came back."

"Not a moment too soon, it seems. You really do have to show him who's boss, Lumina. Otherwise he'll play hell with you."

Leaving her angels sitting patiently, my friend drops their leads and walks in an upright fashion towards Scud. There, with one finger extended in stern fashion, she orders him to release his prize. This time, he does so without hesitation. It is only when she collects it from the lane that she realizes what she's holding.

I watch Petra drop the bone as if it's just delivered an electric shock. "We have to get him home," I say.

Scud whines pleadingly. With the yellowing relic before my beagle once more, I fear he might just take it and run. Petra appears rooted to the spot. Grimacing to myself, I collect the bone from the ground and fling it back into the cemetery.

It's only as the bone switches through the air that I realize what I have done.

"Leave it, Scud!" I yell, as my dog yields to his instincts. With the flies giving chase, I watch him tear through the gates and vanish between two gravestones. "We're not playing fetch!"

To my relief, Petra finds the presence of mind to order him back. She does so with great authority and a lot of volume. For one horrible moment, however, it looks as if Scud is too far gone to return. I breathe a sigh of relief when my beagle slopes back onto the path carrying nothing with him. I only wish that the flies would give up on their quarry as he has.

"Your dog may have the power to revive road kill," says Petra, eyeing the cemetery warily, "but as no resident here has risen to collect their missing bone, I think we can be sure Scud is unable to bring humans back from the dead. Thankfully, it seems this problem is restricted to the animal kingdom."

I look at her side-on. "Forgive me, but that doesn't make me feel any better."

"You need to be strong, Lumin. An air of panic has swept this spa town." She stops there and pulls a face as the last of the flies catch up with my dog. "If he'll kindly regroup with my angels, we can be on our way."

I peer down at my beagle, and prepare to add some weight to my voice. "You heard the lady," I say. "What are you waiting for?"

It is rewarding to see Scud obey my order without delay. I only wish that he would do so with a little more grace.

"Oh, for *goodness* sake!" Petra sounds exasperated when my dog bounds wildly towards her beagles and causes them to scatter. It prompts her to press her thumb and forefinger to her lips.

"I'm sorry," I say helplessly. "He's always been a free spirit."

This time, it seems only a shrill whistle can halt the chaos Scud is causing. At once, all the dogs stop yelping and await further instruction from their mistress. In response, Petra looks only at my beagle. "Scud," she says, sounding calm but assured, "be nice."

My friend need say no more. She simply gestures at her angels to gather round him. They do so with some reluctance. Even my poor dog seems aware that not one of them is prepared to brush against his flanks. Still, as soon as Petra has gathered their leads in one hand, the pack serves to shield the only beagle that could so easily stand out from the crowd.

"Let's go," I say, anxious to be home now. The sun is beginning to settle on the day, I realize. As I know that patrols will be roaming the lanes after dark, I have no desire to dawdle.

Petra walks at a brisk pace, and with most elegant poise. As I am on her good side, it is easy to see why she had been such a successful model. Before long, we begin to pass people on the lane. Judging by the snatches of conversation we overhear, it's clear that word has spread about a badger back from the dead. What's also evident is that much has been lost in translation.

"*They say the beast is radioactive!*" we catch one man claim.

"*I was told it has wings like a dragon,*" his companion adds, and glances at the sky.

Quietly, I am relieved that people are making

99

such outlandish claims. It means that nobody pays any attention to Petra's beagle pack. In the middle of it all, without a lead but hemmed in all the same, Scud appears to be having the time of his second life.

"We've nearly made it," Petra observes as we turn into my lane.

"At least we can be sure that my dog has been thoroughly exercised today," I say, mindful of the fact that he may not be going out again for quite some time.

Up ahead, a new fissure has crept halfway across the cobbles. The steam rising from it obscures the view ahead. Still, what I make out causes me to stop and gasp. At first I think it is a cat scuttling along beside the wall on that side of the lane. Then the beast glances around on our approach. When two glowing red coals light up at me, I realize what we've disturbed.

"The *badger*!" I hiss at Petra, who stops in her tracks like me. "Look!"

Clearly this wretched-looking soul has keen ears. On hearing me, it begins to snarl and growl. I see what look like strings of green drool yawn apart between pointed teeth and prepare to run when its hackles rise. It is only when Petra takes a step forward that this abominable creature shows its true nature by turning tail for the forested slopes beyond the cottages. I must say, for a corpse that had been decaying for some time it is recovering remarkably well.

"We can only hope that in a short space of time nobody will be able to tell it's a zombie," notes Petra, and drops her attention to the dog responsible for breathing life into the poor thing. "Scud's appearance is certainly improving by the hour."

I am not entirely sure I can agree with Petra about this. Flies continue to trouble my beagle, while his collar is now thickly encrusted with little black corpses. At the same time, it is clear that his stitches are ready to be removed. Yesterday, he had looked like he was built in sections. Now, any signs that my father had been forced to sew him back together have very nearly disappeared.

"I don't care how he looks," is all I can think to say. "He'll always be my Scud."

"Your father is a miracle maker, Lumin. Make no mistake."

Despite the air of pride I feel at what he has done for us both, I am uneasy about spending any longer

angels ✓

angels ✗

in the open air. "We should get Scud indoors," I say, looking around now. "I think we have survived quite enough narrow escapes for one day."

We choose to walk around the steaming fissure on account of the beagles. With their bellies so close to the ground, passing over that kind of heat would be uncomfortable. On the other side, I am deeply relieved to find nothing between us and the gate to my cottage. Petra's angels certainly demonstrate their own feelings about completing their task, for they fold away from Scud as one and regroup behind their mistress.

Scud responds by attempting to scratch behind one ear with his hindfoot. It's his bad side, I realize. Try as he might, it means my dog can't quite make contact with the itch. Even so, he doesn't topple this time. What's more, I swear the limb in question is beginning to twist back into the correct position. Before long, I think to myself, it'll be as good as new.

"Your dog has certainly returned to test us," observes Petra. "I believe your holidays may be hard work."

Scud gives up trying to scratch himself. Instead, he looks at me pleadingly. Ignoring the flies, I reach down and scratch his ear for him.

"Things have certainly changed for me," I say, and stand tall once more. "But I'll do whatever it takes to keep him at my side."

I swing open the gate for Scud and watch him hobble through. When I turn to thank Petra for all the help she has provided, I find her gazing at me intently.

"I admire your determination," she says. "I see so much of myself in you."

I take this as a compliment, but then the way she seems to lose herself in thought leaves me feeling a little uneasy. Behind me, I hear the door to our cottage open up. I break from her gaze and look around. When a familiar figure steps out with a beagle in his arms, the one I had picked out from the lab, I turn back to see Petra blinking to her senses.

"Another angel for me," she says with a smile. "Your father really is heaven-sent."

14

The puppy farm is located some way south of the spa town. The road out there is often very busy, for it is used by trucks travelling between the lagoon and the capital. For this reason, my father and I set off at first light in a bid to beat the traffic. I am riding in the sidecar attached to his motorcycle, in matching leather hat and goggles. It's great to hear the roar of the engine and feel the wind on my face.

The only thing missing is Scud.

Normally, he would travel with us. Under the circumstances, we had no choice but to leave him at home. I am not concerned about him for now, however. My father has gone to great lengths to make sure that he is safe and happy. Not only are the cottage doors secured, but my dog now has the means to run off any excess energy.

The exercise treadmill arrived last night. My father had borrowed it from the store beside the spa gym and tipped a delivery driver to drop it off on his way home. Now, if Scud becomes restless, he need not go crazy inside the cottage. Indeed, we had left him getting to grips with the machine. Several times he had tripped over himself and shot backwards so quickly that the flies were left hovering without a host. Still, I am confident he will have mastered it by the time we return. We have even left Petra with the spare key so that she can check on him through the day. It means I am free to look forward to offering yet another beagle the chance of freedom. The chosen pooch might have to put up with a short stay inside the lab, but I know for sure that it will come to no harm.

"It's a shame we are collecting only one!" I yell across at my father over the roar of the engine. "It would be a dream to bring home every single puppy, don't you think?"

My father hears me clearly enough but concentrates on keeping the motorcycle on the road. Despite the early hour, we have just encountered several trucks on their way to the spa. As we pass them by, the buffeting winds threaten to send us into the ditch.

"It would be wonderful to free all the beagles," he shouts back, having veered momentarily into the dusty verge. "But for now we must do it the only way we can."

By the time we reach the track leading up to the farm, it is a relief to be off the road. The first thing we approach is a checkpoint. The guard on duty in the booth sees us coming. We are familiar faces here, and so he simply tips his cap and hauls back the lever to raise the barrier.

The track is made of concrete. Weeds spring from the cracks and choke the verges. My father slows considerably to negotiate the ruts and potholes. The big, windowless building that looms into view looks like something that has been plucked from an industrial estate and abandoned out here. All I can say is that a great deal of money has been spent on the perimeter security, but next to nothing on the grounds or the puppy farm itself.

As soon as we pull up outside the main entrance, my father kills the engine and peels away his helmet. For a moment, we listen to the muffled sound of dogs barking and howling.

"We're a little too early," he observes, and gestures at the padlock. "Though not soon enough for the poor dogs in there."

I have nothing to say in reply. The din from the

beagles inside this enormous shed speaks volumes. As the baying begins to rise on account of our presence, I feel an ache from deep within. I have to blink back hard to stop my tears from spilling.

Climbing out of the sidecar, I face up to this imposing building. What's most striking is the absence of any windows. There are spaces built into the upper reaches of the breezeblock walls but only to keep the air circulating. They offer only a glimmer of natural light to the occupants. It's as if the place has been designed to taunt and tease them with a hint of what life is like on the outside.

"This is not right," I say to myself.

My father finds a flask of water from the bike's store box. He takes a swig and hands it across to me.

"Some would say that bringing Scud back from the dead is a greater crime," he observes. "We all have different reasons for doing what we believe is best."

Kicking at the dirt on the ground, I think about what he has said. "Petra Appollonio believes you are a miracle maker," I tell him. "She is stunned by how swiftly his scarring has healed."

My father smiles to himself. "The secret is in the preparation of the mineral mixture," he tells me. "It is not something I had ever concocted before. Nor do I intend to ever again. Should Doctor Grubo discover what I have done, he would surely force me to hand over the formula. Just imagine what he would try to do with it!"

Behind us, the sound of someone clearing their throat prompts my father and me to glance at one another and freeze.

"Am I disturbing?"

I recognize the gruff voice before I turn and see the man himself. The dogs inside the building certainly know who it is, for they fall into a cowed kind of quiet. Grozo Pongratz grins at me, revealing

GROZO PONGRATZ

several gold back teeth. It's the only glittering aspect of the puppy breeder. In his grubby overalls and rubber boots, and with his wild, thinning hair pulled back into a tight pigtail, Grozo is the most disturbing person I know. I am also aware that wasn't what he meant when he cut into our conversation.

"You surprised us," I say.

"Seems so." Grozo scratches himself as if his underwear is made of wool. He then flicks his gaze across to my father. "You say you've brought your beagle back from the dead? That sounds like shady work, Mister Lupesco. The kind of move that could put me out of business. If every laboratory in the country could revive their test dogs when things went wrong, there'd be no need to replace them with nice new puppies."

At first, my father seems quite lost for words. "You mustn't believe everything you hear," he offers eventually.

"Maybe," replies Grozo Pongratz flatly.

This time, I am with my father in finding no words to slide out of this fix we are in.

Grozo narrows his eyes, considering us both. Then he blinks and bursts out laughing. "I'm joking with you!" he admits, and spreads his huge hands. "A resurrected dog? I've never heard such nonsense! That spa town of yours

111

must have steamed your brains. What planet are you living on?"

Chuckling still, Grozo produces a key from the pocket of his overalls. My father and I stand aside as he reaches for the padlock. We exchange anxious glances as he works to unlock it. "Are you ready?" he asks, and prepares to push open the double doors. "Welcome to *my* world."

15

The puppies have been kept in darkness throughout the night. With a flick of a switch, Grozo Pongratz lights up an overhead strip light. It blinks on from one end of the building to the other. At once, I find myself looking at what appear to be a thousand and one little beagles adjusting to the glare from their cages.

"I trust you little devils behaved yourselves

overnight," says Grozo, addressing the puppies here. "Now be nice and stop mewling. We have some visitors!"

Stacked six high in facing rows, the imprisoned puppies are a sight which tugs painfully at my heart. I feel this way every time I come here. I know my father is equally appalled. He looks up and around, but Grozo does not notice how his eyes have become glossy. Sometimes I wish that I could peel away the roof and the walls to this place, cut through all the cages and set every last dog free. That is just a dream, of course. People have tried to break into this puppy farm, but the security here is so tight that nobody has got beyond the perimeter walls.

Nobody but us, I am proud to say. Which is why we are only able to rescue these poor things one beagle at a time.

It isn't the perfect solution. As Grozo simply breeds more dogs to replace those that leave, it might even be seen as futile. For my father and I, both humble people, it is the best that we can do.

"If you'll excuse me for a moment," says Grozo. "It's feeding time at the zoo." The puppy breeder crosses to a table with a stack of stainless-steel bowls on top. The industrial barrel of dog food beside it looks quite unappetizing. When Grozo pops the lid and jams a trowel into the contents, the smell confirms my fears. "By rights, this is a chore for my staff on the early shift," he adds. "They're late again, and you don't want to be here when they finally show up." In silence, we watch him slop the first scoop of meat in jelly into a bowl. Then he glances around at us, looking most amused with himself. "Let's just say they're in the doghouse with me."

"May I see the beagle that has been here the longest?" I ask.

"Cage 54C," replies Grozo, with his back turned to us once more and his head sunk between huge shoulders. "She's a live wire, so watch your fingers."

My father and I follow the walkway, scanning the code on each cage until we find the one in question. We always take the longest-serving puppy at the farm. It is only fair and also stops us from leaving feeling plagued with guilt for not choosing any other.

"My goodness!" I whisper, as my eyes fall upon the young beagle inside. The dog, a female, responds by pressing her paws to the bars of the cage, eyeing me eagerly. "She's a *beauty*!"

"Be careful," my father warns, as I reach through with my fingers to touch her wet nose. "You heard what Grozo said."

"She won't harm me," I reply under my breath, and smile as the puppy nuzzles my finger. "How could she when all we'll show her is love?"

I turn to my father. He knows how strongly I feel about saving these dogs.

"Very well, Grozo," he calls across the warehouse, "we'll take this one. How much do you want for her?"

"I think you know the answer to that, Mister Lupesco." The puppy breeder continues to spoon out the dogs' breakfast. When he turns to face us, he does so with a mischievous gleam in his eye. "What price is life, eh?"

I feel my chest tighten and struggle not to seem rattled by what he has said. All of a sudden, it seems as if the puppy farmer is toying with us. It's clear he heard every word we exchanged about Scud's resurrection. I just couldn't be sure whether he really has dismissed it as too fanciful to be believed. Looking tense now, my father produces a roll of banknotes from his pocket. Doctor Grubo has strict limits on how much he is prepared to pay for each beagle. If it exceeds the budget, my father quietly makes up the difference.

"Take the puppy and wait in the sidecar," he instructs me, and looks darkly at Grozo Pongratz. "I believe I may be about to pay a high price."

16

On the journey back to the spa town, our new passenger sits with me in the sidecar. I keep my arms wrapped around her, but she makes no effort to get away. I even suspect she is enjoying the ride. Her tongue lolls from the side of her jaw, flapping in the wind like a sock on a washing line, and a look of sheer joy fills her eyes.

My father shakes his head when he sees that we are bonding, and I know why. We have an agreement about the beagles. Until they leave the lab, we have decided that it is best not to give them names. On the slow transformation from Grozo's devils to Petra's little angels, we must simply care for their basic needs. Anything more is too painful, not only for us but also for dogs who must consider their home to be an underground laboratory.

I remind myself of this as we beetle along the main road. Instead of petting the dog, I study the dark clouds that always seem to close rank around the mountains.

Then I find my father glancing darkly in his wing mirrors and wonder what storm is brewing in our wake.

I turn to see a car some distance back. Unlike the trucks that have encountered us in their path, the vehicle makes no effort to overtake. It simply hangs back, travelling at our pace.

"Is it following us?" I ask.

"Hard to be sure. All I know is, that car was parked at a picnic stop shortly after we left the puppy farm. As soon as we passed, it pulled out in our wake."

I glance behind me once again. The car is gun-metal in colour, squat in shape and looks quite clapped out. It is no different from any other vehicle on the road in this region, which makes me wonder if my father is mistaken.

"Let us find out for sure," he says.

A few miles up the road, as we approach a road-side cafe, my father indicates to pull in.

Sure enough, the car behind us does exactly the same thing.

"What can they want with us?" I ask, and tighten my grip around the beagle.

My father does not respond. Instead, he slows in preparation to peel off. At the top of the slip lane, the cafe looks like the kind of place that has been serving the same breakfast for the last fifty years. The windows are decorated with strings of plastic national flags, but all of them have faded in the sunlight. There is just one car parked outside. The front bumper is marked with the paint from

119

numerous scrapes, as if the driver is prone to attacks of road rage. I imagine the vehicle belongs to the chef. All in all, what with the car on our tail, I do not think it is a good idea to stop here.

"Hold on," my father says, and swings onto the slip lane. I wonder what on earth is going on here. It is only as we near the car park, with the tailing car climbing the lane behind us, that he makes a surprise move. Veering sharply, we find ourselves barrelling diagonally down the slope towards the main road once more. The puppy is alone in finding this tremendously exciting. She even barks as we weave through a narrow gap in the sapling trees that mark the edge of the road and fishtail back onto the tarmac. There is no way the car can follow us. I try to see who is behind the wheel as they race across the car park for the exit lane, but we are travelling too fast.

"They'll be back on the road in no time!" I say.

My father hunches over the handlebars now, concentrating hard. I look ahead, see a junction for a road that leads

through the
woods and real-
ize where we are
heading.

"I suggest we
take the scenic
route," he says, as
we leave the main
road once more.

The detour we have taken
is winding, with plenty of
blind corners and ridges. A
motorcycle is well suited
to this terrain, even if it
does rattle my bones in
the sidecar. By the time
I am quite certain we
are no longer being
trailed, I can focus
on stopping myself
from being thrown
this way and that.

What I cannot shake is the thought that we are being hunted. I try not to dwell on it too much. Instead, as we follow this forested trail, I look out for wild pigs and turkeys. Whenever the beagle spots one, turning tail into the trees, I struggle to stop her from leaping out in pursuit. "Settle down," I instruct her. "Believe me, it isn't nice being chased."

"We don't have far to travel now," my father points out, as the trail crests high enough for us to see over the tree line. The hilltops are the first thing I recognize, along with the tips of the chimneys from the power station below. I may not be able to see the clinic or the spa town, but the steam setting sail from there confirms that we are well on our way home. I would feel a sense of relief, but my father chooses to mark the moment by squeezing a little more speed from the motorcycle. Concerned, I look across at him.

"What did that car want with us?" I ask him finally. "Is it about Scud?"

My father is really motoring now. As we take a hairpin, following the gentle descent towards the spa town, I even feel the sidecar lift away from the ground.

"The sooner we are back at the cottage, the better," he says, on negotiating the turn. "We may have lost that car by taking the forest route, but the main road back is quicker."

17

I hold my breath on reaching our lane. By now, I fully expect to see that car parked outside the gate to our cottage. In my mind, I have pictured the police, with a priest, perhaps, and government officials, waiting for my father. I am braced for him to be charged with crimes that have never been committed before. I will protest, of course. Scud is my life, as my father knows. To bring back my beagle shows how kind at heart he is, but I know they will not listen.

And so it comes as a huge relief to find no sign of the car in question.

My father pulls up and kills the engine. The pair

of us exhale long and hard. Having stopped off at the spa and settled the beagle with her brothers and sisters in the laboratory, he had torn home so fast I really feared the worst.

"Everything is exactly as it should be," I say, and remove my helmet and goggles. "We can relax now."

As I speak and turn to face the cottage, I realize I may have spoken in haste.

"Petra!" My father is first to acknowledge the woman waiting at our front door.

All the blood has drained from the good side of her face. "I have some bad news," she says, clutching at a handkerchief. "Some bad news, and it's all my fault!"

"What ever has happened?" I ask, hurrying up the path now. "What is wrong?"

"I dropped by a little earlier, as I had promised, to check up on your dog." By her tone, I think she is about to tell me that Scud has passed away again.

"Where is he?" I ask, increasingly concerned.

My father is at her side now. He places a comforting hand upon her shoulder.

"I have let you down," she says, dropping her gaze to the path.

"Petra?" My father seems most concerned.

She looks at us in turn. "I unlocked the door to let myself in," she says. "The next thing I know,

124

Scud shot out like he'd been trapped inside with a poltergeist!"

I note the front door is still ajar. I cannot believe a ghost is in residence. I do not believe in such things.

"What has got into that dog?" This time, my father sounds alarmed. "I've never known him to be so spirited."

"Scud raced away so swiftly I had no chance to catch up. I have searched all his usual haunts, from the spa grounds to the square and the graveyard. He is nowhere to be seen."

Across town, several beagles can be heard barking over the steady whisper of escaping steam, but that is not uncommon here. Even if Scud had found his voice once more, I suggest he would more likely be sniffing out road kill.

"You know how inquisitive he can be," I say. "All dogs are like that. They'll bury their noses into any old rotting corpse. It's just unfortunate that a mere nuzzle from Scud brings them back to life."

I am about to press my father for a plan of action when a distant shriek takes my breath away. I face him now with the same air of dread displayed by Petra Appollonio.

"By the sound of things," he says gravely, "I believe Scud may have been successful in his mission."

125

The scream we had heard proves to be infectious. Within minutes, we hear cries and screeches from all over the spa town. The noise even draws people from their cottages. I see a neighbour trot out with a hunting rifle, and that's when I start to feel sick.

"Please don't let Scud come to harm," I urge my father under my breath. "We have to find him, *fast!*"

"But where do we begin to look?" asks Petra. "I have searched this spa town high and low!"

"Then we try again," I say, and march back to the lane. There, I find that some of those who have left their homes to investigate are looking up at the sky. I follow their line of sight, cupping my hand to my brow. It is not unusual to see birds wheeling in the thermals overhead. Of course, the sight of a swan lifting over the rooftops would always raise attention. It's just this one has done so for all the wrong reasons.

It is hard to say how long such a beautiful and graceful creature might have lain dead in the shallows before my dog discovered it. Judging by the bones poking through its decomposing wings, I would guess that it might have been quite some time. The loss of feathers clearly makes it hard for the poor thing to get airborne, while those quills that remain are quick to dislodge as it flaps frantically to get away.

"Having shaken off that car," my father says, standing beside me now, "I had thought the worst was over."

In silence, I watch this shadow of a swan struggle to remain in the air. The way it flies into the sun, you would think the downy trail that flutters back to earth had been fixed in place by wax.

"When Scud returns home," I say, "he's in big trouble."

As I say this, my neighbour lets off a round of buckshot at the swan. I am grateful that he fires wide, but worry that a target without wings might be easier to hit.

"Frankly, it will be a miracle if your dog makes it back in one piece," observes Petra, standing with us now.

I turn to look at my father but find his focus is fixed on a point much further down the lane. The way that his expression darkens prompts me to turn and gasp. On seeing my dog lope towards us, I feel a surge of relief. I am also deeply alarmed. For Scud is on a makeshift lead. It's fashioned from a skipping rope, one that must belong to the spa gym. Then my attention turns to the figure clutching the free end with both hands.

"Does anyone know who this beast belongs to?" Gertruda Gašper looks most irritable as people shake their heads and stand aside for her. "If I find the owner, there'll be trouble."

Scud looks a little sheepish, I think, but most striking of all is his health. He's no longer moving so awkwardly, the sulphurous stench has cleared and, without stitches, he looks much more like a living, breathing beagle. He's still wearing the fly collar, but it seems the infestation is over. All except for the slightest glint in his good eye, he shares no resemblance to the wildlife we have seen resurrected around here. Scud may have been responsible, but visibly at least his face no longer fits the crime.

"Where did you find him?" asks my father hesitantly.

"This *hooligan* hound broke all the rules in the book and trotted right into the clinic." Gertruda sounds thoroughly disapproving. "I was going through reservations with the receptionist when he came up to the desk and even put his paws upon the counter."

I glance at my father.

"He didn't lick your face, did he?" he asks.

I think about what this might mean. Would a slurp from Scud turn a healthy human into the living dead? I look into the masseuse's eyes, searching for that blood-red glint, only to jump when she snaps at us.

"Of *course* he didn't lick my face! I know where dogs like this have been!"

"Oh, I don't think you do," my father mutters under his breath, though he stops himself right there when Gertruda asks if we can identify the dog.

"We tried to shoo him away," she adds, "but he kept coming back. What with so many sightings of demon badgers and satanic swans, it isn't safe for any pet to be roaming freely." She stops there, before softening her voice to address me directly. "At the very least, we wouldn't want him to follow in Scud's footsteps and run into the path of a van."

"Indeed not," I say nervously.

Gertruda looks down her nose at my beagle. "Judging by the fact that it's missing one eye, I would suggest this dog has had a lucky escape in the past. The owner should be thankful, if only I knew who it was. I've been to the four corners of the spa town. Nobody has any idea. I even asked Doctor Grubo," she adds, and locks her gaze upon me. "He suggested you might be able to help."

I feel my heart turn cold as she says this. Despite Scud's swift recovery, I felt sure his missing eye would mark him out to the community as a different dog. Now I fear that Doctor Grubo might've looked into my beagle's one remaining orb and recognized his soul inside.

"I have never seen this dog before," my father says, drawing Gertruda's attention away from me,

"but we would be happy to take care of him until the rightful owner steps forward."

He extends his hand to take control of the makeshift lead. In response, Scud begins to wag his tail. This time, the bones that had been so badly mangled do not make a sound. Even the exposed tip has sprung new hair growth, much like his coat as a whole. I feel so proud of what my father has achieved. Certainly, Petra is looking at Scud in wonder. Only Gertruda regards my beagle with an air of distaste.

"You are a very fortunate canine," she says, addressing Scud now. "Frankly, I am surprised Doctor Grubo did not instruct me to have you put down."

I feel like covering Scud's ears at this terrible suggestion. As it is, they twitch on hearing yet another howl of fright away towards the spa. It is a wearily familiar sound to me now. I can only imagine that yet more locals have spotted some long-dead carcass showing signs of life. When my beagle looks across at me, with an air of guilt about him, he must see the weight of the world on my shoulders.

"If you'll excuse me," I say, and take the lead from my father, "I really should get this dog inside."

My chest tightens as I turn for the cottage. After the trials of the last few days, I am well aware that Scud is one very lucky dog indeed. He could have found himself chased out of town, suffered a buckshot hit to the behind or even been put back to sleep for all eternity. Just thinking about his narrow escapes does little for my anxiety. For I fear his luck might soon run out.

Everyone knows that a cat has nine lives. Clearly my beagle has more than one. The question in my mind as I escort him inside is how many Scud has left.

18

Unlike my dog, I cannot sleep that night. While Scud looks like he's curled up and died at the foot of my bed, I stew between the sheets.

I am relieved that he is back here with me. I am just not sure how long we can keep his identity to ourselves. His enthusiasm for taking off can only mean I will struggle to stop the secret of his existence from slipping out.

The activity across the spa town does not help matters. Before I took to my bed, the number of road kill roaming freely had rocketed. The sighting of the badger and the swan was just the start. When the flattened polecat peeled itself from the cobbles, it was said to regain its shape with one life-affirming gasp. By all accounts, the rotting fox that tore through the square was what had caused widespread panic. Some said a tyre print was clearly visible across its hindquarter, but most were concerned by the blazing gleam in otherwise coal-black eyes. As a result, not one foot patrol but *four* had set out in a bid to track them down.

With daybreak just a distant dream, I peer out of my bedroom window to the front of the cottage. From there, I can see torch lights sweeping across the lanes around the cemetery and out towards the clinic.

"Oh, Scud," I say to myself, "what have you done?"

Behind me, my slumbering dog responds by breaking wind. I crinkle my nose. Scud's fur may no longer stink of bad eggs, but the smell that momentarily consumes my bedroom reminds me how bad it had been. I still find it hard to believe how much his appearance has improved. From his coat to the tone of his muscles, he almost looks as good as new. A matter of days ago, my father had hauled his battered corpse from the grave, and now here he was, looking like he'd never left my side.

I am drawn from my thoughts by the sound of some excitement. At the window once more, I see several torch lights in the middle distance racing towards the same point. What with all the rumours about witchcraft being responsible for reawakening these animals and the fear that they are after our blood, it doesn't help that a full moon hangs over the spa town. It may silver the rising steam, but darkness still cloaks the town. So I am surprised to see a vehicle crawling slowly down the lane without its headlamps switched on. I watch as it parks some distance from our cottage, and my intrigue grows when nobody steps out from the driver's side. I can see a figure in the passenger seat as well, but neither makes any effort to leave it.

Then I realize where I have seen this car before. All of a sudden, I believe I know how it feels to be hunted.

♈   ♈   ♈

"They're here!" I rush barefoot into my father's shed to repeat what I have seen. "Have they come for Scud?"

My father is at his workbench. A rack of test tubes stands beside his notebook. Each contains different shades of a creamy blue mixture. The colouring tells me this is mineral extract. What baffles me are the scrawled equations that fill the page.

"Did you lock the back door behind you?"

"Of course," I say, nodding furiously. "I'm not taking any risks this time."

"Then your dog is safe," he replies. "Just as his secret is safe with me."

At this, my father closes the notebook and slips it into the inside pocket of his jacket. "I am trying to understand precisely what I have done," he tells me. "My sole intention was to bring your beagle back to life. That his injuries healed so swiftly has come as a complete surprise. As for his ability to bring back the dead by touch alone…"

As my father lets his words trail off, I am well aware that he is concerned by the consequences of what he has achieved. I am sure that with some peace and quiet he could cook up a treatment to prevent Scud from resurrecting road kill. At this moment in time, however, the only thing on my mind is the car in the lane outside.

136

"I'm sorry," I say, quite without thinking. "I'm responsible for bringing all this trouble to our door."

"Nonsense."

"It's true!" I protest. "When Scud died, I should've grieved for him. That's what you do when loved ones pass away. It feels like your heart has been torn out but, as much as it hurts, you have to tell yourself that things will get better. It's what life is all about."

My father bows his head. We both know I am talking from experience. We just never speak about my mother any more.

"It was my decision to bring him back," he tells me quietly. "I only have myself to blame. But you know what? Despite all the chaos it has caused, I don't regret digging up your dog. When I see the joy he brings you, it makes it all worthwhile." He takes my hands as he says this and meets my gaze again. "Things will get better. For you, for me, for Scud." My father smiles, only for his attention to be drawn by the sound of an engine coming to life.

"The car!" I look up with a start. "That's the *car*!"

"Let me through, Lumin!"

Following my father, I hurry out into the night. With a squeal of tyres, the vehicle in the lane can be heard pulling off. It's enough to persuade my father to rush for the side gate. As he does so, the vehicle accelerates past the cottage. He sprints out

137

into the lane, and I hurry to join him. By then, the car has disappeared from sight. Much to my relief, I can hear my dog going bonkers inside the cottage.

"Whatever they want," my father mutters, and places an arm around my shoulder, "they know where we live."

When sleep finally claims me that night, I am so exhausted that I sink down deep. I do not recall much about what haunted me through to dawn. All I know is that when I open my eyes to the sound of hurried footfalls and excited shouting, it feels like I am back in the nightmare.

"This way! Over here!"

I jump out of bed and rush to the window. Outside, several neighbours have taken to the lane, including the one with the rifle. Scud is at my side in an instant. He lifts his front paws onto the sill for a better look.

"What is going on?" I ask, and then remind myself who I am addressing. A dog back from the dead is one thing. A *talking* hound would be quite ridiculous.

On hearing yet more distant cries, we watch the group in the lane sprint off in the direction of the spa. I glance at Scud. Not only is he looking in fine health, it seems my beagle would dearly like to rush out and join them. His ears twitch and he begins to whine pleadingly, but I have no intention of letting him out of the cottage. I am about to suggest that he works off his excitement on the running machine, when my father appears at the door.

"They say the fox has been cornered," he says gravely. "The fishmonger's errand boy spotted him at sunrise and raised the alarm."

I close my eyes for a moment, feeling helpless and a little guilty. Whenever Scud had come across the fox's remains, I do not believe he possessed any idea of his powers to resurrect. Had he been aware of the persecution it would face, I am sure he would have loped on by.

"The poor thing. This must be a living hell for him."

Outside, from what sounds like every lane in this spa town, the din continues to gather strength. My father winces and presses a palm to his forehead. "I rescue beagles because I cannot stand to see them suffer," he says. "The same goes for any other living creature – even those that are supposed to be dead."

141

"But what can we do?"

My father does not reply. We simply look at one another with the same resigned expression and then turn for the door.

Leaving Scud whining inside the locked cottage, my father and I follow the sound of the commotion. At the town square, we find others doing the same thing. Everyone is funnelling into the lane leading to the spa and the power station. Troublingly, our neighbour is not alone in arming himself. I see no further shotguns, but I can't ignore the fact that several people are carrying sharp-edged hoes and pitchforks.

Eventually, we come in sight of a crowd. This stretch of the lane is bordered on both sides by woodland, but for a clearing on one side which the loggers use to store timber. Here, freshly-cut pine and silver-birch trunks lie stacked inside a cage, ready for collection. It is open on one side but is obscured from view by so many people peering in. If the fox is hiding out inside, its exit is now blocked.

"*It's a grim beast indeed!*" I hear one woman say. "*One that has no place on this earth!*"

"*Then let us flush it out,*" calls another voice to cheers of approval, "*and send it back from where it came!*"

I turn to my father. "This is a *lynch* mob," I say.

142

"What can we do?" My father is mindful not to be overheard as we join the ranks at the back. "If people knew what had brought that fox back from the dead, they'd surely turn on us!"

As we speak, yet more people arrive to swell the numbers. From the direction of the clinic, I notice several staff members taking shape through the steam. When I recognize a figure approach with a well-proportioned frame and a confident swagger, accompanied by the last man I expected to see here, I am torn between appealing for help and turning my back.

By the time I have decided it might be best to keep a low profile, Doctor Grubo has already spotted me. He even points me out to Grozo Pongratz and exchanges words with him.

"Lumina!" declares the spa founder. "This is no place for a little girl. You should be at home making sure your dog does not stray again."

The way he says it, seemingly so knowing, leaves me lost for words. I reach for my throat, as if to soothe the catch that has formed there.

"Doctor Grubo is referring to the one-eyed beagle that showed up at the clinic yesterday." Discreetly, my father steps upon my toes as if to remind me of this. "Isn't that correct?"

The puppy breeder narrows his gaze at my father, hoping to see the truth behind the story. He is standing away from Doctor Grubo, who fails to note his air of suspicion.

"What other badly behaved beagle could I possibly be talking about?" The spa founder spreads his palms wide. "You sprang to mind as soon as Gertruda Gašper brought him to my office."

"I did?"

"With the greatest respect," he says, lowering his voice and clasping his hands before him, "your recently departed dog was hardly in danger of winning obedience awards. I took one look at that rowdy mutt and decided you would show more patience than Gertruda in reuniting him with his owner."

I try to mask my relief on hearing this. Even if Doctor Grubo remains in the dark about Scud's continued existence, the puppy breeder regards me with clear mistrust.

"The stray is resting," I say nervously, well aware that the dog in question is responsible for the mob behind me gathered around the wood cage. "It seems he had a busy day yesterday."

"We may even offer him a permanent home," my father adds. "A half-blind beagle may well have just been abandoned by its owner."

Doctor Grubo frowns at me. "I really would caution against a permanent replacement for Scud," he says. "Pets are nothing but trouble. Would you not agree, Grozo?"

The puppy breeder shrugs. "All I know is that beagles make me money," he says, eyeing me now. "So long as demand from the testing laboratories stays high."

I feel so uncomfortable under the gaze of these two men that I dare not even look at them.

"Grozo here has paid me a visit to review our working relationship." Doctor Grubo addresses my father directly now. "For some unfounded reason, he was concerned that the lab may soon have no further use for his beagles. Naturally, Mister Lupesco, I assured him that in pursuit of spa products that are both safe and innovative your turnover of such hounds for testing purposes remains steady."

"I don't know what I would do without them," my father replies, sounding somewhat adrift.

"There!" declares Doctor Grubo, and turns to the puppy breeder. "I hope this puts your mind at rest. Goodness knows where you got your information from, but it's business as usual around here."

Grozo Pongratz picks at his teeth. "I wouldn't go that far," he offers, and then draws our attention to the scene unfolding in front of the log rack. "This isn't exactly something you see every day, is it?"

Together, we turn to the crowd. It's hard to see what's going on at the front, but several people are on their bellies, poking sticks into the space under the logs.

"I see its eyes," one says. "I swear I see its eyes!"

Grozo returns his attention to us, as if we alone can explain things.

"It seems some hysteria has gripped the spa

146

town," my father suggests with a shrug.

"Indeed." Doctor Grubo taps his temple with one finger. "Whoever started the rumour that these animals have returned from the dead must need their head examining!"

"I quite agree," I say. This time, I dare to meet the puppy breeder's gaze directly. "And *all* creatures deserve to be treated with humanity."

Having found ourselves cornered unexpectedly here, I am at last beginning to think we are set to escape with our secret intact. Grozo Pongratz looks deeply frustrated. It's as if he cannot quite bring himself to repeat what he had overheard between my father and me for fear of ridicule. Doctor Grubo simply stands there grinning with his shirtsleeves folded to the elbow and his hands upon his hips. In a strange way I am unnerved by how calm he seems. I am used to witnessing the spa director lose his cool at the slightest irritation. When a gasp rises up from the crowd, however, all four of us react in the same way by turning to see what is happening.

"It isn't moving!" declares the figure on the ground. "It's crouched there, staring at me!"

"Hook it out! The wicked beast must know the game is up!"

"Very well, I shall do my best."

I am much smaller than the people in front of us. It does not take much effort for me to slip a little further forward for a clearer view. There, I see the fishmonger's errand boy. On his belly, he's busy poking a long baiting pole under the piles.

"We're ready to catch it," says the fishmonger himself, crouching behind the boy with his hands outstretched. "Go on! Give it a jab!"

I am desperate for this mob to back away. What frightens me is that if I speak up now, people will start asking questions. Instead, I clamp my hand across my mouth in horror at what might happen to the fox if it makes a break into their clutches. If the creature looks as decomposed as had been reported, I fear those at the front might be faced with grappling something that won't hold together for long in its scramble for freedom.

I watch the fishmonger's boy reaching as far under the log pile as he can. He grits his teeth, sweeping the baiting pole one way then the other. When he grins to himself, I know he has caught his quarry.

"Got you," he declares, dragging himself and the pole from under the pile. "Here we go!"

At once the crowd moves closer. I am forced forward by a step, but I do not share the groans of disappointment. If anything, I want to laugh with joy.

The fishmonger's boy climbs to his feet looking very sheepish indeed. He unhooks the bedraggled teddy bear from the end of the pole, barely able to believe what he's holding in his hands.

"Is that it?" someone says, sounding almost disgusted. "A child's toy?"

Ruefully, the fishmonger's boy runs a thumb over the teddy's shining glass eyes. "It must've caught the early light as I walked by," he says. "It's an easy mistake to have made!"

Even before he has drawn breath to continue his defence, the crowd begins to melt away. I turn to find my father. I can see he is as relieved as I am. Grozo Pongratz continues to study me as if he is sure I know more about what is going on here. Doctor Grubo simply grins when I catch his eye. Then he offers me a shrug and, for a very brief moment, I wonder if he knew what was hiding under there all along.

On the walk home, an air of bitter disappointment hangs over the spa town.

"Look at everyone," I observe to my father. "They seem fit to kill!"

I am deeply alarmed by how disgruntled people appear. Earlier, they had been so fired up at news that a zombie fox was about to meet its maker for a second time. I saw bloodlust in their eyes, and I did not like it one bit. It made me fear for Scud. If ever word crept out that my beagle was not only the first creature to rise from the dead, but also the one responsible for bringing back the others, I worry they would surround our cottage, smoke him out and tear him limb from limb.

All the way back I brood about the consequences, should the truth escape. On reaching the path to the cottage, I realize with a start that I might be about to find out.

For, on the stones, in a glistening, sticky pool of its own fluid, there lies a dead snail. Its shell has been crushed underfoot, which is easily done by accident, even if it is horrid when it happens. I do not recall stepping on it when we left, and yet that is not what concerns me at this moment in time. My father sees it too and crouches down beside me for a closer look.

"This cannot be," I say in a whisper, but there is no denying what I see.

For a moment, we watch in silence as the snail's cracked and broken shell slowly reforms. Bit by bit, as if pushed out from the inside, fragments crackle and lock back into place. On completion, the resurrected gastropod lifts one eye stem and then another.

As both begin to glow red at the tips, my father and I come to our senses and look up at one another, for this poor creature could only have been brought back from the dead by my dog. It can mean just one thing.

"*Scud!*" we call out together, and rush for the cottage.

As soon as I lay eyes upon the front door, I know for sure that my beagle has not escaped. The splintered panelling tells me it has been kicked in from the outside. Crashing into the kitchen, I look around in despair. Even as I call his name again, I know he has been taken.

"Who would do this?" I turn to my father and spread my hands. "What would anyone want with a half-dead pet?"

My father scans the room. I see his eyes fall upon the table. I look around and see the note. It is pinned to the table by a kitchen knife. I feel my legs go weak at the sight. My father rips the note free. He reads it to himself. As his eyes move from one line to the next, I watch his expression darken.

"I can stop this," he says, and crumples the note into his pocket. "Lumin, you must stay here. I will be back with Scud in no time."

"Where is he?" I ask, hurrying after my father as he makes his way to the front door. "Let me come with you. *Please!*"

Whenever my father acts with such purpose, I know there is no stopping him. He only pauses at the door to inspect the damage once more. Whoever broke in clearly used a great deal of force.

"The lock is useless," he says. "Once I'm gone, I want you to fetch a chair and use it to jam the handle. Is that understood?"

I am shocked by the discovery that my dog has been taken. Now I am scared by what my father is suggesting here.

"Is someone after me as well?" I ask.

My father tenses at the very suggestion. "Do not leave this cottage," he says. "And do not let anyone in."

21

Even with the chair lodged under the front-door handle, stopping anyone on the outside from twisting it open, I cannot settle.

I do not feel safe inside my own home. Then again, my concern is solely for Scud. I want to get out there and track him down. I just cannot go against my father's orders. I keep thinking about how he crushed that note with such determination. He looked to me like a man who knew exactly what had happened here. I wish that I shared the same view, for I cannot think who is responsible. Scud could only have been seized when we left to investigate the sighting of the cornered fox. Both Doctor Grubo and Grozo Pongratz were also witness to the

scene. I had a very
bad feeling about the
puppy breeder, but he could
not have been in two places at
the same time.

"Don't give up on me, Scud," I mutter to myself.
"I will find you, no matter what it takes. I will fight
for you tooth and *claw*!"

I pace the floor, thinking things through. Then I
hear a key slot into the front-door lock. I stop with
a gasp. My first instinct is to hide behind the table.
It's only when I hear Petra's voice that I rush to
answer.

"Lumin? Are you there? I cannot open the door."

As soon as I remove the chair, the door swings inwards. Petra stands before me holding the spare key in the same way that she holds the leads for her angels. She seems surprised to find that I had barricaded myself inside. Then she sees the damage to the door, and concern comes into her eyes.

"Something bad has happened," I say, and invite her to step inside. "Scud has been taken."

Petra thinks about this for a moment. "Taken by whom?" She points to the heavens. "By you know who?" she asks, sounding sympathetic now.

"I don't mean Scud has passed away," I say, and usher her inside. "He's been *taken*. By thieves!"

As I tell her about the note pinned to the table and how my father had taken off, Petra clutches her hand to her mouth looking shocked to the core. "I will stay here with you," she says, "until he returns with your dog."

"But I feel so helpless," I say. "Scud is my life. I cannot sit here and do nothing!"

Petra is wearing a headscarf, which she unwinds now to reveal the scarring on one side of her face.

"Have faith," she says, and removes her coat. "I am quite sure that your father will be home with Scud in no time at all. Now, have you eaten? Perhaps I can prepare a late breakfast? We should cook eggs. You're bound to feel better with an egg on your plate."

Before I can tell her that I have lost my appetite, Petra is heading for the kitchen.

"Why don't you set the table for your father as well?" she suggests. "I'll even make extra for Scud!"

I am grateful to Petra for her concern. Until I know that Scud is safe, however, I cannot settle. I sit at the table out of politeness, but the scrambled egg she prepares remains untouched. When yet another distant shriek pierces the silence between us, I know that I must act.

"I am going to search for them," I say, and scrape back my chair to stand. "You can stay here, or you can join me."

Petra regards me for a moment, before setting down her knife and fork. "Where will you look?"

I draw breath to tell her that I shall begin with the lanes. Then I think about the turn of events this morning and look her in the eye.

"Can you ride a motorcycle?" I ask. "There is somebody I should like to visit who may well know where we can find them."

22

The ride out to the puppy farm is hair-raising – and not just because of the trucks.

At first, Petra Appollonio seems a little wobbly. I do not complain. Instead, I grip the edges of my seat inside the sidecar and hope that my friend quickly finds her confidence. I see only her good side as she clings to the handlebars. Petra is a beautiful woman, no matter which way I look at her. I only wish that she could see that for herself.

"Keep your head down," I say as we peel off the road and halt at the security barrier. "I am a familiar face with the guards."

Sure enough, the man on duty inside the booth does not even leave his stool. As soon as I lift my goggles and wave, he responds with a nod and lifts the barrier for us.

"I have heard much about this place," observes Petra on pulling up outside the windowless building. "It looks as sinister as all the stories say."

I agree with Petra, but my attention is

159

directed at one of the vehicles parked here. "That's the car!" I say, keeping my voice down low. "The one that has been following us."

Petra removes her helmet and shakes her long hair through. "Then it seems like we have come to the right place."

I turn to the building. By the sound of so many puppies yapping and yelping, Grozo Pongratz is not likely to be among the farm workers inside. Otherwise, we would hear nothing but a tense silence. I do not care to think why the dogs are so timid in his presence. Instead, I focus on the belief that coming here will bring us one step closer to finding my father and Scud.

At the main door now, Petra and I exchange glances.

"Are you scared?" I ask. "I am scared but I cannot turn back now."

Petra smiles weakly. "Don't be afraid," she says. "We're doing our best to find them."

I raise my hand to knock upon the door, only for it to open up from the inside.

"Yes?" The farm worker before us appears most unwelcoming. He's wearing overalls and rubber boots, just as Grozo had. The man does not sport the pigtail, beard and bulk of his boss, but he shares the same steely gaze. Immediately, in a bid to hide her scars, Petra turns away from him. He sniffs

160

noisily, clearly holding back a runny nose. Even so, I cannot help but think he is smelling us. Given the huge fork in his grasp – greasy with dog-food jelly – we seem to have interrupted feeding time. "Do you have an appointment?" he asks, and wipes his nose on his sleeve.

"We picked up a puppy from here yesterday," I say.

"Even if it's faulty we don't do refunds," he cuts in before I can suggest I have only popped back for the paperwork. "If you're after a replacement, you'll have to pay."

Petra turns to face him directly. He looks a little startled, but I am proud of her courage. "That's fine by us," she says. "So long as you have the beagle we're looking for."

Narrowing his eyes, the man switches his attention between us. Then, on hawking up what sounds like a wad of phlegm from the back of his throat, he steps to one side. "Take your pick," he says. "Let me know if you find the one you're after."

Inside, as the caged dogs come into view, I see Petra's expression turn to one of quiet distress. There are at least a dozen workers in here this time. Once again, my friend is careful not to draw attention to herself.

"So this is where my angels start out in life," she whispers, looking up and around. "If only we could do something for them now."

"We do what we can," I remind her. "My father makes sure these dogs taste freedom eventually. I just wish I could say the same about Scud."

At the far end of the building is a storeroom. The door is closed, but light can be seen through the gap underneath. When a shadow sweeps across from within, I know for sure that the room is not empty. Petra notes it too, and together we move in that direction. Several workers are busy collecting bowls of dog food from the figure with the fork. None show any affection towards the dogs. At every cage they shove in a bowl and slam the hatch closed before the poor thing inside can even blink. I see Petra wince at the sight. I fear she might intervene and attract the wrong kind of attention. Instead, she pauses before a cage as if we really are here to pick up a puppy.

"I won't let you down," she says under her breath, though I am unsure if she is addressing me or the beagles behind the bars.

I glance over my shoulder. Those workers delivering the bowls of dog food are now working their way back towards the serving table.

"Keep moving towards the door," I hiss, and push her onwards. "If they're being held anywhere, it has to be in there!"

As we approach the last cages in the row, I prepare to take matters into my own hands. I look round to check that I am not being watched, glance

162

at Petra and then break for the door. I twist the handle, only to find that it is locked. At once, my heart fills with disappointment. I look around at Petra, then come round full circle on hearing the sound of a key turning.

"Lumina?"

I gasp and take a step away. The puppy breeder is the last person I expected to find here. He steps out after me and closes the door behind him. He seems much bigger than I remembered. Immediately, the puppies fall quiet.

"You surprised me," I say, quite genuinely.

"It seems you weren't the only one." Grozo Pongratz looks around at the cages. "These hounds have no brains. All I have to do is lock myself away to run a stock check on tins of slop and they think it's safe to make a racket."

"They're dogs," says Petra, drawing his attention. "You can't switch them on and off."

"Indeed not," he agrees, without shifting his gaze from me. "Though if your father is to be believed, they can be *restarted*."

I feel my heart flip when he just comes right out with it. Any story that I might have spun to explain why we are here vanishes from my mind. All I can do is face up to the puppy breeder and ask him an honest question.

"My father is missing," I say. "And Scud has been

163

dognapped! Do you know where they are?"

Grozo Pongratz takes a moment to digest this. At first, his bushy eyebrows bunch together. Then he sighs to himself, and his entire expression clouds. When he bellows at two members of his workforce to join us, I fear that Petra and I are about to be held captive ourselves.

The pair who approach us are solid-looking fellows. Each has a barrel chest and stubble you could strike a match across. I glance at Petra, who shares my concern.

"They don't look very friendly," she observes.

"Meet the Borbély brothers." Grozo scratches lazily at his tummy as he speaks. "Mark my words, little Lumina, they're in big trouble."

I face the puppy breeder, just to be sure I had heard him correctly. The way he is frowning at the two men now makes me wonder what they have done wrong.

"You promised me you wouldn't let me down," Grozo growls as they draw up beside us. "I wasn't asking for much."

The brothers glance at one another but appear mystified. Grozo sighs to himself, as if he's in some pain, and then pinches the bridge of his nose. He bows his head, eyes closed.

"Is everything all right?" I ask.

"No, it is *not!*" Such is the puppy breeder's explosion of anger that I wonder if he has been sharing some of Doctor Grubo's medication. At the same time, I am very glad it isn't directed at me. The Borbély brothers shrink from their boss, but there's no stopping him now. "I asked you to keep an eye on Mister Lupesco and the hound. It was a simple instruction, so what went wrong? All you had to do was follow them home, watch the cottage and step in if anyone tried to seize them! Clearly that was a task too much for you clowns. Now, get out of my sight! You make me sick to my stomach. Look at you. You're lucky I don't bring up my breakfast all over your boots. You're *useless!*"

Throughout this outburst, as the brothers make their exit, I turn my attention from Grozo to Petra and back again. "You sent them to *protect* us?" I ask when Grozo falls silent. "Protection from *who?*"

The puppy breeder takes a moment to regain his composure. He sighs to himself, as if preparing to make a confession.

"When I overheard your father claim to have brought Scud back from the dead, he swore that he would never share his secret. Now that's fine by me. If every lab began to resurrect their test beagles I'd be finished."

"But you didn't believe a word he said," I remind him. "You laughed it off!"

"I did," he agrees, "but then I considered what kind of man I was dealing with. Every time he purchased a pooch from my farm, your father has always been honest and fair. You wouldn't believe the number of clients who come through this door, poke at my puppies and try to buy them from me at the lowest price possible. They're always claiming this one is sick or that one is lame. Your father was the only one to look me in the eye and pay the asking price. He's an honest man, Lumina."

"You can certainly trust him," I say.

"Which is why I decided to send a couple of my people to watch over you all." Grozo Pongratz shakes his head despairingly. "I wanted to be sure nobody would try to prise the secret from him. Now he's gone missing, along with your dog, it could well be that demand for box-fresh lab beagles like mine will wither and die."

"Then some good will have come from this," mutters Petra under her breath.

The puppy breeder smooths back those course stray hairs that have slipped from his pigtail. "I'm sorry," he says, after quite some time, "who is the lovely lady?"

"I run a rescue home for beagles," replies Petra, and introduces herself. "A sanctuary from the suffering caused by the likes of you!"

Before Grozo can react, I steer the conversation back to the subject that matters most at this moment. "So, if Scud and my father aren't with you," I say, "who is behind their disappearance?"

"There can only be one person," mutters Grozo. "I think we all know who."

I face Petra. She swallows uncomfortably.

"Doctor Grubo?" I say out loud, for I can think of nobody else.

"I visited him this morning to find out whether he knew anything of Scud's resurrection. Naturally, I didn't breathe a word and, though I found no firm evidence, I left with more questions than answers. Just what is happening in your spa town, Lumina? Are these rumours of rancid, reanimated road kill connected to your dog?"

"It seems so," confirms Petra. "But don't be alarmed. The creatures touched by Scud make a miraculous recovery. Within days, you wouldn't know any of them had once been corpses rotting in ditches."

As she speaks, I think back to this morning's encounter with the doctor and the puppy breeder. Having rushed to the woodcutter's clearing, I believed Grozo Pongratz was the greatest threat to the dog responsible for raising the poor fox from the grave. Now I find myself dwelling on what had been hauled out from under the timber and realize how wrong I had been.

"The teddy bear," I say, barely able to take in what I am thinking. "It was placed there deliberately, wasn't it? Doctor Grubo must have known my father and I would be drawn to reports that a fox had been cornered. Which meant Scud was alone in the cottage."

"He was late for our meeting at the clinic. Arrived in a sweat, now I think about it." Grozo pauses there, reflecting on what this means. "Then again, we all know how the doctor likes to exercise."

I catch Petra's eye. She smiles sympathetically. "Even if the doctor has your dog, I am sure he would not harm it," she suggests.

"The dog is of no use to Doctor Grubo." The puppy breeder paws at the back of his neck as if discomforted by what he has to say. "What he's after is the formula your father created that brought him back to life. By seizing Scud, Doctor Grubo has given your father no choice but to hand it over. Either he shares his secret, or …" Grozo Pongratz trails off to draw a finger across his throat, "your dog returns to his resting place."

Immediately, I prepare to plug my helmet back on my head. "We must get to the clinic as fast as we can," I say, and then face the puppy breeder directly. "Will you help us?"

Grozo Pongratz examines his nails. They are in dire need of a cut and clean. "You want your dog back. I want to be sure no more lab beagles return from the dead to destroy my business." He stops there and grins at us both. "That means we want exactly the same thing."

24

We elect to take the fastest
form of transport back to the spa
town. The motorcycle allows us
to make quick progress, but it isn't so
easy for Petra Appollonio – not with the
puppy breeder riding pillion.

"Don't keep pulling in to let the trucks pass,"
he yells over the din of the traffic. "Be brave!"

My poor friend looks somewhat unsettled with
such a big, unwashed beast of a man issuing instruc-
tions from behind her. That he's wrapped his hairy
arms around her waist can't
help her concentration.

It's certainly a bear hug I would not wish to experience myself. Judging by the way her nose has crinkled, Petra is more concerned by what's behind her than by what lies ahead. Still, it's good to know we can back up our bid to rescue Scud and my father with Grozo's physical presence.

As the power station and the spa loom into view, there in the distance beyond the crest of the road, we are forced to steer around the flattened corpse of a hedgehog. All of us eye it warily. I am relieved that it does not stir when we roar on by. To be quite sure, I even turn in my sidecar seat and watch it shrink into the distance. Facing the front once more, I breathe out in relief and then focus on the task at hand. Whatever obstacles we face, I am prepared for anything.

"At last," says Petra, when we reach the main square. A plume of steam greets us from the geyser, rising high up into the air, but we do not stop to admire it. Indeed, as the steam evaporates, I am surprised that my friend is brave enough to drive straight through. "The direct route," she says and hunches into the headwind. "The sooner I can get this passenger off my back, the better!"

"That's no way to talk," replies Grozo. "I have feelings!"

"So do your puppies," she says. "But now is not the time to discuss it."

By now, Petra has made my father's motorcycle her own. Despite the extra load, she rattles over the cobblestones on our approach to the spa gates. It is only as we race past the woodcutter's clearing that I suggest we slow down.

"We must think of Scud," I say. "If we rush in and alert Doctor Grubo to our presence, he might lose his cool and act rashly. I do not wish my dog to pay the ultimate price. Not *again*, at any rate."

"Lumina is right." Grozo Pongratz taps Petra on the shoulder, as if he is in charge here. "We shall go in quietly and use the element of surprise."

Once through the gates, Petra steers the motorcycle slowly into the parking bay. There are many vehicles here. All are the same gunmetal-grey colour. The only difference is in how dirty each of them is. Grozo is the first to climb off, much to Petra's relief. As ever, blankets of steam rise up from the lagoon. It is hidden behind a ridge of volcanic rock, but nothing can mask the sulphurous smell. Over the growl from the power station, the sound of gentle splashing tells me there are people in the healing waters.

"Are we ready?" Grozo gestures at the main doors. "Lead the way, ladies."

I feel very tense as we approach the doors. With no way of knowing where Doctor Grubo might be hiding out, along with my father and my dog, it is vital that we do not draw attention to ourselves.

Petra must pick up on how I'm feeling, for she places a reassuring hand upon my shoulder. "We're in this together," she says, and even acknowledges the puppy breeder looming behind her. "Whatever it takes, you'll see your dog again."

Her words are enough to spur me on. I am first to step inside and greet the receptionist. She smiles back at me, but it seems to freeze across her face when her attention turns to the pair behind me. Petra's scars might sometimes cause people to stare, but I suspect in this case it is the sight of the big man in the overalls and rubber boots. I know Grozo Pongratz has made many visits to the spa, but like everyone who provides a service I realize he is expected to use the tradesman's entrance.

"He's with me," I say breezily. "It's OK."

The receptionist relaxes at this, but I don't. Not when my words draw another figure into view. She rises to her feet from behind the desk and sets down the papers she's been filing. "No, it most certainly is not OK." Gertruda Gašper holds out her hand. "May I see your membership passes?" she asks, and snaps her fingers. "Nobody goes beyond this point without a membership pass."

Facing her now, I begin to wonder whether the masseuse deliberately hides when visitors arrive in the hope that they'll try to flout the rules. Thankfully, I have my membership card to show her, and so too does Petra. What troubles me is the manner in which she glares at Grozo.

"There is a side door for people like you," she says, looking down her nose at the puppy breeder. "I should also remind you that we don't accept trades-men without prior appointment. This morning, you called ahead of your meeting with Doctor Grubo. Kindly do the same thing now."

When Gertruda gestures with her fingers for Grozo to turn around and leave, I fear we might have lost him. Anxiously, he looks at me and then at Gertruda Gašper. "But I am here for a soak in the lagoon," he says, and clears his throat. "A soak, a sauna and maybe even a massage."

"A *what*?" Gertruda looks horrified. I presume this is at the prospect of laying her hands upon the puppy breeder's ample, unwashed flesh. Flustered now, she reaches for her appointments folder. "I'm afraid the massage room is fully booked," she says without checking. "As for the soak and the sauna, that's for members only."

Grozo Pongratz reaches for his wallet. "Then it's about time I joined," he declares.

I glance at Petra, who winks at me. Gertruda,

meanwhile, appears to have run out of any further reason why the puppy breeder cannot enter. "Very well," she says with great reluctance, and finds a form for him to complete. As he scrawls out his name and address, Gertruda returns her attention to me.

"What are you waiting for?" she asks. "Run along and get changed. Just be sure to shower before you step into the lagoon." She pauses there and leans away from the unusual figure currently hunched over the paperwork she has given him. "You'll find the same facility in the men's area, Mister Pongratz," she informs him. "Please make good use of it."

"But—" I draw breath to say that we're not here for a soak, only for Petra to cut across me.

"We're on our way," she says, and pulls me away by the wrist. "Grozo will find us in the water."

25

I step out into the open air,
wearing only the spa's regulation swimsuit and cap,
and take a sharp intake of breath.

Under less pressing circumstances, I would relish
this moment between leaving the changing room
and wading into the warm, aquamarine waters.
Even if sleet was to begin blowing in sideways,
there would always be a thrill in facing the elements
before taking the plunge.

"I feel terrible," I tell Petra, who joins me in the
lagoon now. "My father and Scud are missing, and I
choose to unwind."

177

Petra does not respond for a moment, and I know why. In such a comforting environment, all you can do is sink up to the neck and close your eyes. There are some half a dozen bathers in the lagoon. Everyone keeps themselves to themselves, enshrouded in steam and cocooned in their own private bliss.

"We had no choice," my friend offers me eventually. "This is the only way we could get past Gertruda. She's even watching us now. Over there. *Look!*"

Sure enough, on turning discreetly, I see her face in the viewing gallery. She's standing behind the glass with her powerful arms folded across her chest and a look of some disdain.

I turn back to Petra and suggest we move out of her line of sight. The silted floor always feels strange underfoot. It seeps between my toes as we move behind an outcrop of rock and into the shadow of the great power station.

"She really is unhappy about Grozo," I say, "but if my father and Scud are in trouble, his presence will be invaluable."

As I share this, I hear a gasp from a nearby bather. Lately, I have heard many people sound as startled on witnessing road kill rising from the dead. On this occasion, I look at what has waddled out of the men's changing rooms and wonder which is more alarming.

"Hey, ladies!" Grozo Pongratz spots us through the steam and gives us a cheery wave. He's wearing a towel around his waist, which is partially obscured by his overhanging belly. When he disrobes, dropping the towel to the ground, I cannot help but shrink and turn away. It's only when I peep back around that I see he is at least wearing the spa's regulation briefs. "Is it warm? I'm coming in!"

There are no signs around the lagoon forbidding jumping and diving. It is simply accepted that anyone who comes here will respect their fellow bathers. So when the puppy breeder takes a run-up to the edge and launches himself into the water, it is no surprise that he is greeted with howls of protest.

"For goodness sake, Grozo!" I am furious with the man as he wades towards us. Such is the impact of his entrance that a sizeable wave now fans out across the lagoon. "We're supposed to be keeping a low profile!"

"You'll get us thrown out!" adds Petra, who can barely bring herself to look at a man with so much curly ginger chest hair.

"It's all part of the plan," he says, only to face the viewing gallery when Gertruda calls out his name.

"Your antics have not gone unnoticed," she warns him through the window she has opened. "Consider yourself under observation."

When Grozo turns to face us once more, he is grinning with satisfaction. "She's watching *me* now," he says, "but not you two."

I mull over what this means, turn to Petra, and then share his smile. "He's on to something," I say. "We just need to find the right time to slip away."

Petra peers over the rocks at Gertruda. My friend

180

seems pained by our predicament. "The door to the sauna is right behind her," she notes. "She is expecting us to steam following our soak. I do not see how we can possibly slip from her attention."

Petra's outlook leaves me feeling trapped all of a sudden. Unless we can get around the masseuse, who might as well be standing sentry, there is no other way to access the rest of the clinic. I am convinced that Scud and my father must be here. I feel it in my bones.

"Then what we need," suggests the puppy breeder, who weighs onto his back with his hands behind his head, "is a *grand* distraction."

Grozo — help or hindrance ?

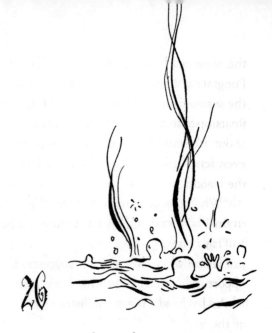

26

"Are you quite sure about this, Lumina? I am worried about whether his presence here is really helping."

Petra and I creep out of the changing room, having dried ourselves and dressed as quickly as we could. Together, with bated breath, we make our way towards the viewing gallery. As it curves around the lagoon, it is easy for us to remain hidden from Gertruda's view. She is still at the window with her hands clasped behind her back and her attention fixed on one individual only.

"There he is," I whisper, and gesture at the figure in the water.

A light breeze has arisen outside. Through

the steam now drifting across the lagoon, Grozo Pongratz continues to make his presence known to the surrounding bathers. Unlike everyone else, who floats serenely in the healing waters, he's splashing about like a man drowning in slow motion. He's even scooped up handfuls of silica from the bed of the lagoon and applied it as a face pack.

"What is he doing?" asks Petra. "We didn't agree to this!"

"He's certainly enjoying himself," I say. "It's just a shame he won't allow his puppies the same opportunity."

As I speak, Grozo Pongratz notes our presence at the window. He offers me a sly thumbs-up, and I know that our moment to slip by Gertruda has arrived. As discussed, Grozo rises to his feet. Waist-high in the milky blue waters, with his head upright and his belly sucked in as best he can, the puppy breeder raises his hands to the sky.

"This isn't going to be pretty," says Petra, taking a deep breath at the same moment as I do.

Outside, in the lagoon, having flipped into an unsteady handstand, Grozo Pongratz's pale and podgy legs can be seen scissoring the steam. Gasps of horror and howls of disgust greet the move, not to mention the fact that his regulation briefs are now visible above the waterline. Further along the

gallery from us, Gertruda Gašper throws open the window once more.

"You are a hooligan, Mister Pongratz! An unwashed and ill-mannered hooligan! Please leave the lagoon immediately!"

Upside down in the water and unable to hear the instruction, Grozo Pongratz does a remarkable job of remaining on his hands. He even manages to walk them along the floor of the lagoon, much to the dismay of several elderly bathers in his path. When Gertruda bellows his name again, leaning out of the window now in a bid to be heard, I know that we must make our move.

"Doctor Grubo's office is just beyond the sauna," I say. "We must act quickly!"

I try to make as little sound as possible, creeping forward at first and then picking up the pace as we prepare to skirt behind the masseuse. I can barely breathe, such is my fear that she might catch us and throw us out. I know she would not listen to my protests. In fact, if I pleaded that I was here to rescue a dog she presumed to be dead, I would be out on my ear within seconds. Mercifully, as we approach the masseuse it is Grozo who continues to be the subject of her rage and indignation. Through the corner of my eye, I catch him surface and then gasp for air. Much of his face pack has washed down into his hair. With his pigtail and folds of flesh, it leaves him resembling some terrible mistake of a merman. Now that Gertruda has his ear, it buys us enough time to make our way behind her unnoticed.

"This is outrageous behaviour! Kindly exit the lagoon, you unmannered oaf!"

On hearing this, delivered with unbridled fury, both Petra and I break into a run. I am first to reach Doctor Grubo's door, which I throw open without knocking.

"Where is my father? What have you done with Scud?" I am so fired up it isn't until I draw breath that I realize the doctor is absent from his desk. He is nowhere to be seen, in fact. We are alone with his bodybuilding photographs and the rowing machine.

"What now?" Petra closes the door behind her

and then leans her back against it. "We're trapped in here."

"One moment." I take myself around to the doctor's desk, searching for clues. A neat and tidy man, he has left an arrangement of sample bottles for spa products beside the jotter. The pencil lying across it might be freshly sharpened, but the violent doodling on the page suggests to me that he must wear it down on a regular basis. My hand moves to the drawer – the one in which I had spied the medicines. Unlike the door, I find it to be locked. Beneath the desk, in the bin, I spy dozens of empty pill canisters. Next, my attention turns to his diary. Judging by the doctor's appointments, he was indeed busy with Grozo this morning. The thick line struck through the rest of the day tells me one thing only. I look up at Petra, who is watching me intently. "Either he's taking time out," I say, "or he's on unofficial business."

Outside the office, from some way back down the viewing gallery, we can hear Gertruda Gašper reprimanding the puppy breeder once more. From what we can make out of his response, it sounds like he's pushing her to the limits of her patience and beyond.

"One session in the sauna," he can be heard to say. "I'm hoping it'll help to dry out the phlegm that keeps

186

building on my lungs. Do you have a bucket I can use when I'm in there, or shall I just spit onto the coals?"

"Kindly exit the lagoon, get dressed and leave. We have no room for antisocial ruffians here!"

"But as a spa member I have a right to steam after a soak!"

"Mister Pongratz, don't make me come in there, pick you up by your back hair and throw you out! I have physically ejected bigger men than you in the past. Make no mistake, as a seasoned masseuse I am adept at bending bodies to my will!"

"Why is he trying to anger her?" Petra looks most unsettled. "I rather wish we hadn't brought him with us. He's hardly helping matters."

"Oh, yes he is." I leave the desk, returning to the door. "He's buying us time. As long as we can hear Gertruda, we know exactly where she is, and right now, that means we're free to slip out of here unnoticed."

"But this is trespass, Lumina, and we both know how quick-tempered Doctor Grubo has become lately! Whatever medicine he is taking to strengthen his muscles is doing few favours for his mind. If he catches us, I am afraid it will enrage him. It isn't safe to go further!"

As I grasp the door handle, it is evident to me that Petra Appollonio is experiencing a slide in confidence. I am scared. Not just for us but for the

187

two things in this world that I love more than anything else.

"I understand if you want to stop here," I suggest. "Your angels need you at home, but without Scud and my father I have nothing. I will not give up until I have found them."

Petra listens to me without comment. Her eyes begin to gloss and for a moment I think she might cry. Finally, she nods to herself, and I know she has made up her mind. "I cannot leave you, Lumina. Lead the way."

go, go, go!!!

27

On the stretch to the steps leading down to the laboratory, we pass several staff members.

I smile at the acupuncturist and also the rare-tea lady with her trolley. At any other time, I would have been happy to accept a cup from her. Following a soak, there is nothing better than to sip a jasmine infusion before entering the sauna. She seems surprised when I politely decline her offer. Petra simply keeps her head down, avoiding all eye contact.

"You're so beautiful," I tell her, having noted how she covered the scarred side of her face. "You just have to believe in yourself."

To my surprise, I think that Petra really might begin to weep. She looks so fragile somehow and avoids my eye. Then she clears her throat, gathering her composure, and alerts me to the red velvet cord strung across the top of the steps. "If we go any further, we really are out of bounds."

I step right over the cord, and invite her to follow me. "Nothing's going to stop me now."

Petra gestures along the last stretch of the viewing gallery. "Shouldn't we check out the caretaker's store first?" she asks. "You never can trust the caretakers."

As I consider her suggestion, a muffled bark from somewhere in the labyrinth of lab rooms below halts me in my tracks. "Listen!" I say. When the next bark shrinks to a whimper, I prepare to descend the stairs. "That's my beagle!"

"*Wait!*" Petra calls out to me so forcefully that I spin around in surprise. She looks at me pleadingly, but I cannot fathom why. "Is this wise?" she asks.

I look up at my friend, there on the top step, and find it hard to recognize her. She looks so different to me all of a sudden, as if perhaps she might take flight at any moment. Eventually, on hearing yet more howls, I break from her gaze.

"I have to do this," I say, and turn to head down the staircase, "whatever the consequences may be."

As I approach the swing doors below that lead into the laboratory, I hear Petra's feet on the steps behind me. I smile to myself, despite my rising fears about what I might find down here, and peer through

NO
ADMITTANCE

the window into the laboratory. Normally, I would see several of my father's colleagues at work at the benches. Instead, the test tubes and the gas burners stand idle. There is not a soul in sight, which is odd, I think to myself.

"Doctor Grubo sent everyone home for the day." Petra looks in over my shoulder. When she says this, I glance around in surprise.

191

"How can you be sure?"

"He'd jotted it down on his pad," she adds quickly. "I noticed it in his office."

I can hear other beagles barking now. It sounds like they're being held in the same place. Despite the labyrinth of rooms, from testing bays to decontamination showers and mineral-extraction zones, there is only one place where I suspect I might find my dog.

"This way." I push through the doors and head for the corridor directly opposite.

"Where are we going?" asks Petra.

"To the beagle pens."

"Be careful, Lumina. Watch your step."

As we push through one room after the other, the sound of barking becomes clearer. When a familiar voice rises into the mix, my chest starts to tighten with fear.

"Do you hear that?" I ask. "Doctor Grubo is down here. I knew it!"

I cannot make out what he is saying, but he sounds irritated. As we close in on the door to the room containing all the dogs, I decide to crash in and hope the surprise works to my advantage. I reach for the push bar across the door, only for Petra to close her hand over mine.

"Wait. There is something I have to say."

"Not now," I hiss, and shove my shoulder into the door.

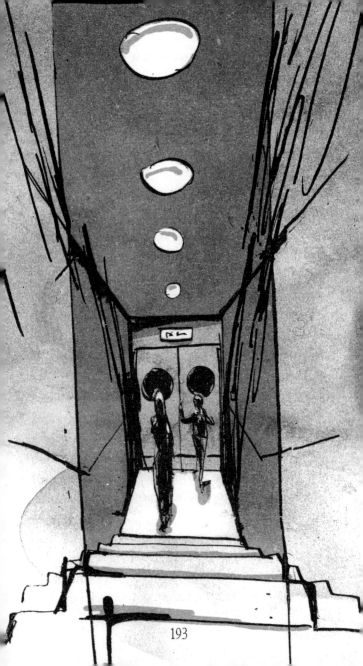

I do so with such force that it swings wide open and bangs against the wall. Before I can take in what we have silenced here, all eyes turn towards us. Not just those of the two figures before me but of all the beagles in their pens. Even our most recent purchase from the puppy farm is in there, looking very unhappy indeed.

"*Lumina!*" My father gasps and snaps away his protective goggles to look at me.

He is standing behind a worktop with an arrangement of connecting cylinders, funnels, tubing and pipes. Something milky is bubbling furiously in a flask above a gas burner. His notebook is open beside it, and the air in here is pungent with the smell of sulphur. Only Doctor Grubo seems relaxed about my sudden appearance.

As for Scud, I cannot be sure what his true response is – the poor thing is contained inside a raised cage so small he cannot move. It's fashioned from mesh and bolts, with an open hatch at the front that's just big enough for his head to squeeze through. As well as having had his collar strapped to the hatch to keep him in position, my dog has been tightly muzzled.

Most alarmingly of all, Doctor Grubo is beside the cage with a large syringe in his hand.

A medicine bottle sits next to a steel kidney bowl on a stand near to him. It contains a black liquid, as does the chamber of the syringe. I do not wish to think what it might do. I just hope that I am in time to stop him from administering it.

"What is happening here?" I turn to my father. He looks pained at my presence.

"You shouldn't have come looking for us," is all he says.

"Wise words." Doctor Grubo sounds unusually calm and confident. He flashes a smile at me. "Everyone knows the difficulties that come from working with animals *and* children." He is alone in chuckling at his own joke, which quickly causes him to adopt a more serious expression. "I'm sorry that it's come to this, Lumina, but right from the start it was clear that your father would not simply share his secrets with me. It meant I had to find a way to persuade him. Seizing Scud and threatening to put him to sleep seemed like the surest way…" He pauses there and draws my attention to the needle. "It was you or the dog," he says, and then tightens his gaze upon Petra Appollonio. "Fortunately for you, Lumina, I was persuaded to choose the latter."

28

I hear Doctor Grubo. I just don't take it in for a moment. When I realize what he has suggested, I turn and stare at my friend.

"You're involved in this?"

Petra drops her head. When she nods, my father and I look at one another in disbelief.

"I'm the one who snatched Scud from the cottage," she admits. "I had a key but chose to force the door open so you wouldn't suspect it was me."

"I would *never* have suspected it was you," I say, feeling as scandalized as I am scared.

"I've been trying to tell you," she says. "I'm just so ashamed of myself."

My father narrows his eyes, as if hoping to see

inside her head. "You're someone who shows such love and kindness to her angels," he says eventually. "Lumina is always saying what a shining star you are. So why would you do such a thing?"

"Why do you think?" Doctor Grubo draws my attention once more, but it is the needle that I focus on. One wrong move from me, I realize, could see him sink the tip into my beagle's neck. Poor Scud cannot even turn his head to face me. He looks so lost, trapped inside that cage. Even the hot coal in his eye seems to burn with a little less intensity than usual. I just hope he knows that I will not give up on him. "What your father has devised is a miracle potion for sure," the doctor continues. "As soon as Petra told me about it, I could see the potential for the clinic."

"For bringing back the dead?" I ask, a little puzzled now and more so when the doctor laughs.

"I have no interest in creating zombie beagles," he says, gesturing dismissively at the dog pen. "I need *fresh* puppies to test my products, and they are in plentiful supply. All I have to do is place an order to receive next-day delivery." Doctor Grubo smiles to himself at this. "If only your father would act upon my request with such efficiency, then all of this could end with no harm done."

I am struggling to understand what is happening here. All I know is that Petra is well aware of *uh oh ...*

what is going on, and so I turn to her. At first she shrinks from my gaze. Then she presses her lips flat and meets my eyes.

"What your father concocted didn't only resurrect Scud," she says. "It caused his injuries to heal miraculously."

"And that is *precisely* the kind of product this spa should be offering our clientele," Doctor Grubo winks at Petra, "beginning with your friend."

Clearly uncomfortable with the attention, Petra presses a palm to the scalded side of her face. Only then do I realize why she has gone to such lengths to force my father's hand.

"As soon as I saw Scud improve so dramatically, I had to find a way," she whispers.

"By betraying us to Doctor Grubo?" I am very angry indeed, and yet I cannot bring myself to let it spill over. Not when I feel such sympathy. "Petra," I say in a trembling voice, "despite all this, I *still* believe you are a kind soul. Through my eyes, it doesn't matter how you look. It's what you're like on the inside that dazzles me about you. It always has done and it always will."

This time, as I speak, tears trail freely down both sides of Petra's face. She doesn't have to tell me that she is sorry. I can see it in her eyes. "As soon as I delivered Scud to the clinic," she says, "I knew it was a mistake."

"Then *why* didn't you say something?" I ask. "You let me travel all the way out to the puppy farm, knowing I would find my dog right here in the lab!"

Petra says nothing. She simply bites into her top lip before mouthing an apology at myself and then my father.

"What Doctor Grubo fails to understand," my father says, "is that I cannot refine the treatment administered to Scud. There is no way of extracting the healing properties from the formula. Essentially, they are an after effect of bringing the dead back to life."

"THEN YOU'RE NOT TRYING HARD ENOUGH!" This time, Doctor Grubo raises his voice so abruptly that I take a breath in surprise. I turn to see his face tighten around the eyes, while the veins in his neck begin to darken and pulse. "You're dealing with a former bodybuilding champion here. In my glory days, the pursuit of a perfect physique knew no bounds! We simply pushed and pushed until the unthinkable became a reality." I imagine Doctor Grubo must have once looked so muscle-bound that he might pop, but I hold my tongue for fear of enraging him further. "Back then, we turned to special medication to achieve our dreams. I see no reason why we cannot offer our clients the same opportunity."

"This medication," my father says solemnly,

"as well as helping to build muscle tissue, did it also mess with your mood a little? In bodybuilding circles, such illegal usage can leave you feeling full of vim and energy one minute, and the next you're thunderously grumpy, with a combustible and even *violent* temper."

"I DO NOT HAVE A TEMPER," he cuts in.

"You wouldn't be using it again, would you?"

"I am ENTIRELY calm!" Doctor Grubo slams his fist onto the table beside him as he says this. It causes the kidney bowl to flip into the air and crash to the floor. The sound, like a clashing cymbal, loads the silence that follows. Awkwardly, the doctor clears his throat. "Mister Lupesco," he says finally, in a voice so quiet it's as if the outburst never happened, "clearly the threat of putting your daughter's dog to sleep is of no concern to you. Otherwise, you'd have found a way to extract what I need from your formula. I'm afraid it leaves me with no choice," he adds, and injects my dog so calmly that a moment passes before Petra wails in horror and I realize what he has done.

"Scud!" I scream, as the beagles in their pens bark and howl. "Scud! *No!*"

29

I cannot believe that Doctor Grubo could be so cruel. Immediately after he has administered the fatal jab, Scud's eyelids grow heavy and his head begins to hang. Finally, with a great sigh, my beloved dog's body falls slack.

"Now, that was quick and painless." Doctor Grubo unstraps the muzzle. When Scud's tongue rolls out, there is no doubt that he is dead. "Another beagle bites the dust," he adds. "Even if he has already had a bite once before."

My father had suggested that the doctor's mood-swings were down to outlawed medication. As I throw myself upon the man, I am driven purely

by outrage at witnessing his savage act. I do not care for my safety any more. With Scud gone, I am nothing.

"How could you *do* such a thing?" I rage, and beat upon his chest. "My father might've gone against nature by resurrecting Scud, but it is *you* who have become the monster!"

At once, Doctor Grubo grabs my wrists. He does so with such power that I gasp and cease my attack. I look up and find him peering at me victoriously.

"Evidently your father needs further persuasion," he says, upon which he spins me around and locks his arm around my neck. "Mister Lupesco, I advise you to redouble your efforts to create the treatment I need. Otherwise," he says, and brandishes the syringe with his free hand, "your daughter will share Scud's fate."

Both Petra and my father seem to freeze for a moment. They simply stand there motionless while Doctor Grubo slots the syringe into the medicine bottle and draws up the plunger with the top of his thumb.

When he turns the tip towards me, it is Petra who is the first to respond. As she steps forward to intervene, I feel the grasp around my neck tighten. I hear Doctor Grubo repeat his threat, which is

enough for her to back away. Even so, he doesn't
slacken his grip, which is so harsh now that I cannot breathe. My father shouts at him to unhand me,
but I might as well have cotton wool in my ears. In

a panic, I feel some pain in my eyes as they begin to bulge. I struggle and wriggle to be free, but the man is too powerful. My fury at what he has done to Scud is entirely replaced by a sense of desperation, but when I glimpse my dog from the corner of my eye, I grasp at a glimmer of hope.

It is a twitch of one ear that I note at first. Then I see my beagle's chest rise with an intake of air. When Scud opens his remaining eye, I witness a glaze clearing like mist from water. There is no burning ember behind it. All I see is my dog, pure and simple. Doctor Grubo continues to scream at my father. Then he screams for a different reason entirely – when my dog swings around to clamp his unmuzzled jaws around his upper arm.

"WHY WON'T THIS BEAST DIE?" Doctor Grubo bellows in anguish, and fights to be free from Scud. My beagle's body might be imprisoned, but he refuses to release his quarry. I even see several bolts and pins pop from the cage, such is his determination to hang on. "Get him off me! Get this demon away!"

As Doctor Grubo tugs in vain to be free, I seize my own opportunity to break away. Immediately I run to my father, who hugs me to his side. Petra joins us. Together, we look on as Scud resists all attempts to force him to let go. When another bolt snaps from the cage, all three of us step back by a pace.

"Any moment now," my father breathes, as the

sound of metal buckling joins the growling and the cursing, "your dog will be free."

Sure enough, it is the cage that gives up before my beagle. I see one mesh panel then another crack apart, before Scud releases his grip upon the doctor and bursts from his confines.

"Good boy!" I cry, but for once he pays me no attention.

"Get your mutt under control!" Doctor Grubo demands, only to fall silent as my beagle lowers his head, flattens his ears and growls. It is an unbroken and menacing rumble, and one that is quickly backed up by all the beagles in the pen. Hearing this, the doctor begins a slow retreat to the door. "Good doggy," he says, in as friendly a voice as he can muster, and then gestures over his shoulder. "You're free to leave."

Scud responds by curling his slack black lips and snarling. At once, looking truly fearful for his own safety now, Doctor Grubo wheels around and flees from the room. Before I can stop him, Scud reacts by giving chase.

"Come back!" I yell, and not just at my dog, yet both disappear from view.

The beagles in the pen step up their barking and baying at this. Had Petra not then rushed across and opened the gate, no doubt they would've torn it down.

"*Fly*, my pretties!" she cries, as they flood from the room. "Go hunt him down!"

I turn to my father. He is staring at the apparatus in front of him.

"Scud cheated death," I say. "Doctor Grubo put him to sleep. I saw it with my own eyes, and yet he came back again. Have you made him *immortal?*"

"Far from it." My father tears the top page from his notebook. It is filled with scribbled calculations that go way beyond anything I could hope to understand. With a knowing grin, he holds one corner to the flame from the gas burner. It blackens, burns and turns to a tissue of ash. When he releases the remnants, a moment before the flames reach his fingers, they float upwards with all the grace of an angel returning to heaven. "Doctor Grubo did not kill your dog just then," he tells me. "He simply put the zombie to sleep."

"And brought the real Scud back to this world?" I think about this for a moment, and then a grin spreads across my face. "You must've known that would happen!"

"When I first resurrected Scud I did not fully understand the science," he says. "That he has been reanimating road kill simply by licking their lifeless bodies was certainly an unexpected side-effect. It was also somewhat troubling. So I've been reviewing what I did throughout his recovery. It was my conclusion that the only way to rid his system of the unwanted elements of his revival would be by killing the zombie within."

I gasp when he says this. "So why didn't you do that earlier?" I ask.

My father smiles and shrugs. "Do you think I could even *temporarily* put your dog down? Besides, I couldn't be completely sure Scud would come back to us."

Petra has been listening to our exchange from the door. She still looks remorseful and yet, at the same time, it's clear she's itching to follow the pack of beagles. It sounds as if they're running riot in pursuit of Doctor Grubo.

"I think we can safely say that Scud has bounced back good as new," she says. "But unless we catch up quickly, I fear he might be looking to settle a score."

30

It is not hard to track down the beagles. The racket they are making leads us swiftly through the laboratory area and then up the stairs. What we find at the top, however, leaves me fearing that the trail has gone cold.

"Where is Doctor Grubo?" I ask out loud. "And where is Scud?"

The dogs from the pen look lost. Some are pawing desperately at the glass windows overlooking the lagoon, while others have slipped through the changing rooms and now stand at the water's edge,

barking wildly. I know that
I would recognize Scud among
them, but I see no sign of him.

Instead, and more pressingly, we
are faced with the sight of a most irate masseuse.
That Grozo Pongratz is nowhere to be seen tells
me Gertruda must have lived up to her threat and
thrown him out of the spa. Given the sheer size of

the puppy breeder, I am left thinking she will make mincemeat out of us.

"Who let the dogs out?" she screams, from the far end of the viewing gallery. *"Who let the dogs out?"*

My father pays her no attention. His focus is locked on the lagoon. "Doctor Grubo has fled through the water," he says. "He's tried to shake Scud off his scent, though I don't suppose it will have stopped him. That beagle looked deeply determined."

"So where are they now?" asks Petra, but already I have spotted a likely escape route.

"They went that way." I point towards the far side of the lagoon. There, in the shadow of the great power station, a set of steps is cut into the lava rock. Rising up from the water, it allows bathers a chance to cool off at the edge should they wish to take a break from their geothermal soak. Looking at it now, I realize the steps also lead to an inspection walkway that skirts the power station and the steaming pipework that encloses it. Both Scud and Doctor Grubo could have vaulted the fencing that prohibits the bathers from venturing further, giving them access to several service doors from there. I waste no time in sharing my thoughts with Petra and my father. "He's hiding out in the power station," I say. "That's no place for my beagle. There's heavy machinery in there!"

212

My friend looks pained when I point this out.

"I feel so terrible about what has happened," she says. "You must believe me when I say that I had no idea Doctor Grubo could be so cruel."

"We have to stop him," I say. "By any means!"

"That might not be so easy." My father gestures over my shoulder. I turn to see Gertruda thundering towards us.

"First I have to banish a layabout from the lagoon," she bellows, "and now this! Mister Lupesco, these beagles are your responsibility! They belong in the laboratory. This is a clinic, not a kennel. By letting them out you have contravened *every* rule in the book!"

"Is there a law against being a battleaxe?" my father asks, so vocally that Gertruda cannot fail to hear.

In response, the masseuse snarls and rolls up her sleeves. The meaty forearms she reveals look mighty intimidating as she marches towards us. Judging by her mood and pace, she might just sweep us all into her ample bosom and boot us collectively into the car park. I look to my father, seeking some guidance.

"If anyone is going to get hurt here," he says with a sigh, before reaching for the window and pushing it wide open, "it might as well be me."

ツ   ツ   ツ

213

I am the first to splash into the warm and milky water. Petra is next to clamber out, landing waist-high next to me. Above us, we hear the sound of a scuffle. Then Gertruda appears at the window with my father in a headlock.

"YOU CANNOT ESCAPE FROM ME," she cries at us. "Once I've dealt with your father, I will hunt you down!"

"Go!" he yells from the crook of her elbow, before the masseuse hauls him away. "Do what you can, Lumina!"

I look to Petra, feeling lost without him all of a sudden.

"He will find his way out," she assures me. "Your father is a resourceful man."

Together, we begin to wade through the water. The beagles on the rocks send us off with a barrage of barking, while a scattering of baffled bathers look on through the steam.

"I have never been inside the power station," I say. "Ever since I was little, I have been told to stay away."

"For good reason," Petra replies. "One wrong step and you face a drop into the boiling magma."

Despite her warning, I am determined not to let Doctor Grubo escape with Scud. My shoes fill with silica and my clothes are wet through. Even so, I will not let my dog down now. Midway across the lagoon, however, where the floor shelves gently away to allow people to swim freely, I realize my friend is no longer at my side.

"What is wrong?" I ask, on turning to find Petra at a standstill. She looks torn, and I think I know why. "You can't swim, can you?"

"I have never waded out this far," she says. "Now I feel like I've let you down for a second time."

With no time to spare to find another way around, I tell her she can hold her head up high.

"I know that you are with me in spirit," I say. "Just as I am with my dog."

"Please be careful!" she calls out, as I turn and push out across the water. "You're dealing with a man who is close to losing his mind!"

I am breathless by the time I crawl out to the steps. For a moment I remain on my hands and knees, then take a breath and scramble to the walkway. There, despite feeling the cold in my sodden clothes, I try the first steel door. On finding it locked, I race to test the next one along. It opens inwards with a squeak. At once, I am greeted by a wall of billowing steam.

"It's like an oven in there," I mutter to myself, and cover my face to step inside.

The hot, moist air takes my breath away. At once, my clothing begins to steam. The light inside is sparse, but once my eyes adjust, I find myself looking up and around in awe. For the building itself is really only a shell. I'm looking at a web of overhead walkways, all of which are arranged around the vast cylindrical structure that occupies the centre ground.

It's the size of a windmill without the sails, plastered in dials, valves and levers, and sprouts piping

216

like the legs of a spider. A deep hum comes from within. I see steam swirling up into the overhead extractor fans. The blades reflect an intense glow from below. It takes a moment for me to realize that this must be coming through boreholes in the rock – for the magma layer is under our feet here, a sea of fire that we have come to depend upon for power, heat and light.

More importantly, I see no sign of life in here. My eyes flit from one walkway to another. In the looming silence, I begin to worry that Doctor Grubo has given me the slip. With my heart quickening, I head towards a flight of metal stairs immediately in front of me. As I make the climb, and my view opens out, I am aware that the clanking sound my shoes make gives away my presence. Then, from across the building, I hear a growl, followed by urgent footfalls, and realize it is not me who should be so worried.

"Doctor Grubo?"

My attention is raised to a walkway that runs crossways from where I am. It leads to the upper reaches of the cylinder, where it divides to encircle the structure. I see a figure make a break across this bridge. The column of steam he races through makes it hard to be sure who it is. Then again, I only need to see the beagle in pursuit to know I have found our man.

get him

31

I have never seen Doctor Grubo look so desperate. I also note that his shirt tails are in shreds. So too is the seat of his trousers.

"Call your devil of a dog off!" he cries out, on spotting me below. "He means to kill me!"

"He wouldn't harm a fly!" I reply, though it does seem as if Scud has made an exception here.

I see no hint of zombie in my beagle, and yet he tears after the spa owner with unbridled ferocity. Such is Scud's pace that Doctor Grubo is forced to scramble from the walkway and up onto the cylinder rim. Scud leaps at him, jaws snapping, spittle spraying, and only misses because the doctor tucks his legs away. Then I think about what lies on the other side of the rim and realize that I have to help.

"That's enough!" I call out to Scud, but he pays me no attention.

Doctor Grubo is up on his feet now, balancing unsteadily on the lip of this great cylinder with both arms spread wide for balance. Desperate to get across, just to pull my dog back, I race up the next flight of stairs. I am high enough now to see just over the cylinder rim. As well as the pipes crawling up the interior wall, I make out two horizontal strengthening struts. They fit across the top of the cylinder, crossing at the centre. Even before Doctor Grubo edges around to the strut nearest to him, I know what he has planned. It may be a sure-fire means to get away from my dog, but I am concerned what might happen should he slip.

"I don't think that's very sensible," I shout across the gulf between us, but already the spa director is edging his way out across the furnace below.

"I am safer here than at the mercy of your beagle!" he yells back, sounding ragged around the edges now.

Just below him, Scud continues to jump, scrabble and scrape at the side of the cylinder.

"Doctor Grubo, if you'll give me a moment, I will do my best to calm my dog." I scramble up the last in this flight of steps. As soon as I see that it opens out onto a walkway, one that will take me across to the cylinder, I run as fast as my legs will carry me. "Please stop snapping at him, Scud! I beg you to leave him alone."

Midway across, as my beagle continues to ignore my pleas, I find myself drawing to a halt. On several occasions, as I remind myself now, Petra Appollonio has stepped in and shown me how a dog respects authority. With nothing to lose, I stand tall, take a big breath and issue a command that even draws Doctor Grubo's attention.

"*DOWN*, SCUD! Get down this instant!"

Maybe it is my pitch, tone or sheer volume that gets through this time. Whatever the case, my beagle sinks back to his haunches with a whimper before settling on the walkway to wait for me. At any other time, I would praise Scud and tickle him behind the ears. On reaching his side, my only concern is in persuading the doctor to come back to the rim of the cylinder. I find a toehold upon a dial and lift myself up so I can see him. What I find causes me to gasp.

"Doctor Grubo," I declare, "your clothes are smouldering!"

I find him midway across the cylinder. His arms are outstretched like a high-wire artist. The heat up here is incredible. I only have to glance down to know why. Some of the boreholes that penetrate through the rock are so wide I get a clear view of

I SMELL BURNING!

the molten porridge below. I glance back at the doctor, see the ribbons of his shirt tails scorching, and wonder whether he has dared to look down himself.

"I need no distraction at this time," he calls back, when I appeal to him once more. "Your dog means to maul me!"

"Scud is under control. He will not harm you now. I give you my word!"

Doctor Grubo pauses on hearing this. I see his head bow, as if pondering his next move. Then, as thermals of rising heat continue to make his body appear to ripple, this former bodybuilder's shoulders sag.

"Oh dear," he says next, in a voice so quiet I barely hear him. Even before he fills his lungs and appeals for help, I can see his determination has deserted him. "Get me out of here!" he cries. "I'm melting!"

With the heat on my face, I feel quite helpless. I am only small, compared to Doctor Grubo, and do not see what I can do. At the same time, I am not prepared to see the man go up in smoke. He may be twice my size, I tell myself, but I can match him in courage.

"Reach out to me," I say, and extend one arm. "Before it is too late!"

Doctor Grubo peers over his shoulder. I see genuine terror in his flushed face. "I cannot," he whispers. "I do not dare!"

It is seeing his shirt continue to scorch and smoke that urges me to take action. Without further thought, I scramble onto the rim. As I do so, I catch sight of a door at the far end of the building open up to the daylight. A silhouette appears in the frame. I recognize my father's voice in an instant.

"*Lumin, no!*"

Unfortunately, as he races towards a flight of steps, another figure appears behind him. Gertruda Gašper does not pause at the door to look around but thunders in, giving chase.

"You have no authority to come in here, Mister Lupesco! I cannot allow such disrespect for rules and regulations to go unpunished."

For such a stocky individual, the masseuse moves at quite a pace. On the steps, I see her reach out and attempt to grab my father by the ankle. I have not time to wait to see if she succeeds – not with the figure on the strut before me threatening to ignite before my eyes.

"Take my hand," I plead with him. The heat underfoot is intense, but then I do not intend to stay out here for long. "Doctor Grubo, you have to trust me."

Again, the spa director glances over his shoulder. This time, however, as I continue to advance unsteadily across the fiery chasm, he turns and

223

reaches out to me. Another step and our fingertips meet. One more and I clasp his hand.

"Bless you, child," he whispers, like a ghost of his former self, and meets my gaze directly.

The soles of my feet feel as if they are touching hot coals. At first I fear Doctor Grubo will not budge. He is much bigger than I am, after all, but when I try to draw him towards me he responds like a puppy – one shown some compassion, at least.

"Let's go," I say, just as my father reaches the rim behind me.

"I'm coming to get you, Lumin! Do not move a muscle!"

I turn to see my father haul himself into view. Just as he does so, a formidable pair of hands lock themselves upon his shoulders. When Gertruda Gašper clambers onto his back, it's enough to pull

him away from the strut. Her face is contorted with rage. She does not once glance across the cylinder. I am unsure if she is aware that Doctor Grubo and I are even out here.

"Must I tear your limbs from your sockets?" she yells in my father's ear. "How *dare* you disobey me!"

Watching my father struggle with the masseuse, I realize I am quite alone. I switch my attention back to the doctor. He looks so distant and detached.

"Follow me," I say. "One step at a time."

After a moment, with a blink, Doctor Grubo appears to come back to me. He nods, his lips tightening, before placing one foot in front of the other. I turn back towards my father. He attempts to shake off Gertruda, and though she clings on tight he finds the presence of mind to reach out towards me with one hand. There is some way to go, and he knows it. Seeing only desperation in his eyes, I imagine he must find the same in mine. His lips form my name, but I hear only the hiss of steam and the magma bubbling below. The temperature out here is intense. It leaves me feeling breathless and close to collapse.

Then I pick up on what can only be the sound of melting shoe soles slipping on steel and see my father's face fall.

"LUMIN!"

32

I glance back in time to see the doctor lose his footing. For a moment, I think his balance will recover. Then our gaze meets once more and I know that it is too late. He tries to release his grasp from mine as he drops. All I can do is hold on tight as he yanks me down after him and grab the girder with my free hand to save us both from incineration.

"Let me go, child! All is lost! Save yourself!"

I hear his command, but I do not act upon it. How could I do such a thing? Doctor Grubo is looking up at me from between my flailing feet. Below him, through the pipes, the magma layer spits and bubbles furiously. The heat is so intense that it seers my eyeballs and my lungs. His weight is unbearable.

I feel as if my arm
might just pop from its
moorings.

Doctor Grubo must recognize this,
because he wraps his free arm around my legs
and then releases me from his grasp. This frees me up
to grab the strut with both hands. I am more secure

now, but it does little to ease the load. I am just not built to carry such a weight, especially when it starts to thrash about in a bid to avoid the heat.

Looking back to the rim, I see my father abandon all hope of escaping from Gertruda's clutches. Instead of fighting to free himself, he attempts to crawl out towards me with the masseuse on his back. It certainly takes her by surprise. It's almost as if it serves to burn off the blinkers that have been driving her to uphold the rules.

She looks up with a start, peers down from one side then the other, and shrieks, "Turn around! Take me back! Please don't let me cook like my cottage!"

In a blink, Gertruda switches from wrestling with my father to clinging on for dear life. Unfortunately for me, it only serves to slow his progress. With Doctor Grubo below me, wailing helplessly now, I do not think that I can hold on long enough for my father to reach me. I sense my fingers slipping. Every muscle in my body feels stretched like pastry dough. Then I hear a voice from the opposite end of the strut and cling to one last hope.

"I may have been kicked out before I could take a sauna, but this is certainly enough to work up a sweat!"

I look around to find the puppy breeder, wrapped in the clinic's regulation white towelling gown, crawling out upon his hands and knees.

"Grozo!" I cry. "Help us!"

Behind him, Petra Appollonio appears at the rim of the cylinder. She looks shocked and horrified by what she sees. "Hold on, Lumina! Just a moment longer!"

On his belly now, Grozo calmly reaches down and grabs my wrist. "You know what I need?" The puppy breeder grits his teeth as he prepares to heave. "A long holiday. Preferably somewhere nice and cool."

I am too exhausted to reply. Instead, as Grozo lifts me from the abyss, I concentrate on anchoring myself upon the strut. Once I am secure, he reaches for the man still clinging to my legs.

"Be quick!" cries Doctor Grubo, his clothes smoking wildly now. "Before I melt away!"

With impressive muscle, Grozo Pongratz grasps the doctor by the scruff of his shirt. I hear it tearing and then see it come away in his hand. By then, however, the doctor has hooked his arms around the strut.

"This way, Lumin!" My father is behind me. I am horribly stifled by the heat, and when I feel his hands grasp my shoulder I practically faint into his embrace. As he drags me clear of the strut, with Gertruda still wrapped around him, I feel my eyes grow heavy and then close.

❦   ❦   ❦

When I open them again, stirred by a dog's wet tongue in my face, I find myself back on the walkway that rings the cylinder, slumped in Petra's lap. I blink to regain some focus and find four familiar figures peering down at me.

"Such a brave little girl!" My father beams at me. Even Gertruda Gašper seems reluctantly relieved that I have returned to my senses, as does Doctor Grubo. The puppy breeder is helping the man to stay upright. Judging by the way the doctor is trying to nurse his behind, wincing every time he presses his palms to what is left of his trousers, the searing heat has left its mark.

"The doctor has something to say to you." Grozo Pongratz shoves him between the shoulders, encouraging him to step forward. "Isn't that right?"

Between them, the two men display very red faces from the heat they have endured. The puppy breeder is perspiring in droplets, which he wipes from his forehead with the sleeve of his towelling robe. As Doctor Grubo turns even more crimson, I can only think the man is struggling with what he goes on to share.

"Lately I have not been myself," he confesses, and removes a pill canister from his pocket. The doctor studies it in his palm for a moment, shaking his head ruefully. "Strange how a brush with death is able to change one's outlook on life. At this moment

in time, despite everything, I am feeling remarkably clear-headed and calm. This time I intend to stay that way."

When he turns to flick the canister over the rim of the cylinder, my father smiles approvingly. We hear it rattle down one of the pipes. A brief fizzing follows, matched by a flare of light from within.

Doctor Grubo sighs and shrugs his broad shoulders. "I owe you my life, Lumina. Had you not taken matters into your own hands just now, I would have been barbecued. I am also sorry for the way I have treated Scud. His loyalty to you is something I cannot ignore."

As he speaks, Petra strokes my hair and I cuddle my beagle, who has settled beside me. Scud no longer smells of sulphur at all, I realize. Looking at him now, you would have no hint that he had once been buried. My dog is with me now for life.

"I am just happy he is here," I say.

Doctor Grubo nods and smiles. "Maybe I should take credit for that." He reaches out to pat Scud on the head, only to snatch his hand back smartly when my dog responds with a growl.

"You'll have to earn his trust," I say, grasping Scud's collar just in case. "It might take some time, but Scud knows a good soul when he sees one. Just as I do," I add, and glance up at Petra.

Throughout this exchange, Grozo Pongratz looks

increasingly uncomfortable. "Don't get too sentimental," he tells the doctor. "It's only a beagle, after all. And beagles make good business."

Doctor Grubo looks over his shoulder at the puppy breeder. "Not any longer," he says. "I have been a fool, and I am determined to put that right. The time has come for this clinic to change its business practices. So, from here on out, dogs are banned from the premises."

"At last, some common sense!" Gertruda looks down at me victoriously.

"As indeed are you." The spa director jabs a finger at her. "You're fired."

The masseuse looks at him aghast. "But you can't! I have a contract of employment!"

"Then I shall pay you to leave." Doctor Grubo raises one eyebrow at her. "Enough for you to build a cottage on cooler ground perhaps?"

The masseuse considers this for a moment. "But who will enforce the rules?" she asks. "You cannot manage without me!"

"Sometimes, Gertruda, as Mister Lupesco and his daughter have demonstrated, rules are meant to be broken."

Gertruda Gašper seems lost for words at last. She draws breath to protest, facing us each in turn. Then, with an indignant squeak, she turns on her sensible shoes and stomps towards the exit. "I do not wish to be here for a moment longer," she calls back. "If anyone tries to escort me from the premises, I shall dislocate their limbs and tie them in unspeakable knots."

As she leaves us, I realize Grozo Pongratz is looking crestfallen. While everyone is watching the masseuse, he is staring at the mesh floor beneath our feet. "What about my puppy farm?" he asks Doctor Grubo. "If the spa stops using beagles, others will be sure to follow, and where does that leave me? I saved your life!"

"If needs be, I shall compensate you too," replies the doctor. "Whatever it takes, I do not wish to see any more beagles running around the spa town. We have quite enough as it is."

I look up at Petra and find her sizing up the puppy breeder. Her attitude towards him seems a little less frosty. I even think she is looking at him with a playful hint of warmth.

"Once you've enjoyed your holiday in a cooler climate," she suggests, "perhaps you and I should think about working together. I have no room for any more angels, and, with so many to rehouse, your farm would make an ideal sanctuary."

"A *sanctuary*?" Grozo Pongratz looks my way, finds me grinning at the proposition and breaks into a smile himself. "If the spa has no further need for my beagles," he says with some reluctance, "then I suppose we should go for broke."

"You never know," I add, still weak and slightly scorched, "you might even grow to care for them. After all, what you did just now shows you have a heart."

Doctor Grubo chuckles at this, only to be silenced by a filthy glare from Grozo. He shrinks from the big man, smoke still rising from the seat of his trousers, and draws breath to address my father.

"But what does this mean for your laboratory, Mister Lupesco? We are prohibited from dispatching products that have not undergone rigorous safety checks."

My father smiles, nodding to himself, and then rakes his hand through his hair. "Life must go on, Doctor Grubo, as I have always said, and I think I know how. With changes to the labelling, I predict soaring sales for the clinic's products. At last, we have a means of standing out from the competition. Not only are we able to offer a range that promotes health and vitality to our customers. Now we can promise to clean up their consciences as well."

"But how can we be assured that our creams and lotions won't smart or sting?" Doctor Grubo appears most concerned. My father simply turns to me and invites me to speak.

"It's simple!" I rise to my feet with Scud at my

235

side. He looks up at me with a glint in his one remaining eye. This time, however, it is one of pure devotion. "From here on out," I say to finish, "all products will be tested on *humans*."

life goes on

Acknowledgements

I can be a demanding author at times, and would like to apologize to everyone who has helped me dig up this story. My attention to detail has undoubtedly tested the talented team at Walker Books, as well as Philippa the Fixer. I hope they can forgive me.

Finally, both Quinton Winter and Matt Whyman have suffered greatly for my art. I do hope they'll return my call for the next book I have in mind …

feather and Bone

$\mathbf{K}$amil knows something sinister is going on in the woods.

Deep amongst the trees, the old Squawk Box poultry farm is stirring back to life, but it doesn't seem to be processing chickens, and the villagers are too scared to ask questions. Questions like…

Why is Mister Petri, owner of the Squawk Box, supplying the enormous Cosmina Barbescu with extra rations?

What has the local schoolmistress witnessed at the farm, and how does she keep losing her fingers?

Why is that flock of chickens following Kamil everywhere he goes, and did that rabbit just *explode*?

Together with Flori, the poacher's daughter, Kamil investigates a mystery smelling mankier by the moment.

This is a work of fiction. Names, characters, places
and incidents are either the product of the author's
imagination or, if real, are used fictitiously.

First published 2011 by Walker Books Ltd
87 Vauxhall Walk, London SE11 5HJ

2 4 6 8 10 9 7 5 3 1

Text © 2011 Lazlo Strangolov
Illustrations © 2011 Quinton Winter

The right of Lazlo Strangolov and Quinton Winter to be identified as
author and illustrator respectively of this work has been asserted by
them in accordance with the Copyright, Designs and Patents Act 1988

This book has been typeset in Goudy Old Style

Printed and bound in India

All rights reserved. No part of this book may be reproduced,
transmitted or stored in an information retrieval system in any
form or by any means, graphic, electronic or mechanical,
including photocopying, taping and recording, without
prior written permission from the publisher.

British Library Cataloguing in Publication Data:
a catalogue record for this book is available from the British Library

ISBN 978-1-4063-2345-0

www.walker.co.uk

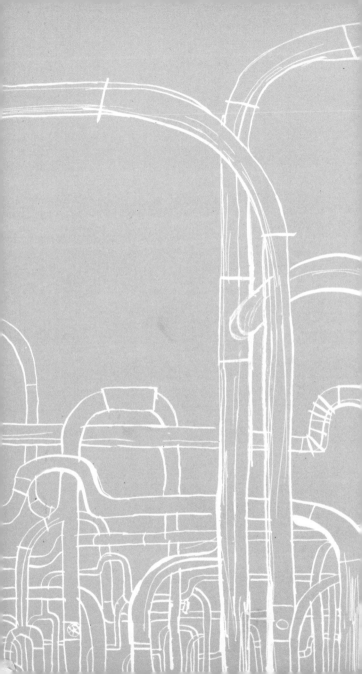